'You want me to be your mistress.'

His head shot up and he reared back, narrowing his eyes at her. 'That's a rather crude way of putting it,' he said stiffly.

'But it's true, isn't it?'

Miles got up from the couch and began pacing up and down the room. She sat there, tense and anxious, watching him, until finally he came back to stand before her, his face grave.

'I just don't see any other way.'

Dear Reader

The first few months of a new year are a time for looking forward and wondering what the future holds for us. There are no such worries when you pick up a Mills & Boon story, though—you're guaranteed to find an exciting, heart-warming romance! This month, as usual, we've got some real treats in store for you. So, whatever 1995 brings you, you can be sure of one thing: if you're reading Mills & Boon, it's going to be a year of romance!

The Editor

Rosemary Hammond grew up in California, but has since lived in several other states. Rosemary and her husband have travelled extensively throughout the United States, Mexico, the Caribbean and Canada, both with and without their two sons. She enjoys gardening, music and needlework, but her greatest pleasure has always been reading. She started writing romances because she enjoyed them, but also because the mechanics of fiction fascinated her and she thought they might be something she could do.

Recent titles by the same author:

BETWEEN TWO LOVES

VOYAGE TO ENCHANTMENT

BY

ROSEMARY HAMMOND

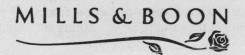

MILLS & BOON LIMITED
ETON HOUSE, 18-24 PARADISE ROAD
RICHMOND, SURREY TW9 1SR

*All the characters in this book have no existence outside the imagination
of the Author, and have no relation whatsoever to anyone bearing the
same name or names. They are not even distantly inspired by any
individual known or unknown to the Author, and all the incidents are
pure invention.*

*MILLS & BOON and the Rose Device
are trademarks of the publisher.*

*First published in Great Britain in 1994
by Mills & Boon Limited*

© Rosemary Hammond 1994

*Australian copyright 1994   Philippine copyright 1995
This edition 1995*

ISBN 0 263 78460 6

*Set in Times Roman 10 on 12 pt
01-9503-50789 C*

Made and printed in Great Britain

CHAPTER ONE

MELISSA looked up from her book and stared out at the blank blue sea, brilliant under a glaring sun. It was only the second day out, and already she felt she'd made a mistake to come on this trip. What had made her imagine that a glamorous cruise down along the Mexican Riviera would somehow transform her from the shy little mouse she'd been at home into—what? She sighed deeply.

'Penny for them.'

Melissa glanced over at Frances Venable, the plump grey-haired woman who sat in the deck chair beside her contentedly knitting, and smiled at her.

'I'm afraid they're not even worth that much.'

Frances set her knitting down in her lap, pursed her lips and gave Melissa a stern look over her glasses. 'You know, dear, you really should get out and mingle more with the young people on board.'

She waved a hand towards the swimming-pool, which as usual was full of squealing young women vigorously splashing each other and tossing a big red beach ball back and forth in some sort of game. They all wore colourful scanty bikinis, and, it seemed, each one had the figure to do them justice. Melissa thought ruefully of her own meagre endowments in that quarter.

'Oh, I was never much good at mixing in with that kind of crowd,' she said. 'In fact, they terrify me. They

5

all seem so confident and self-assured.' She shook her head. 'It's just not my style.' Then she had to laugh. 'Nor do I have the figure for a bikini.'

'Nonsense!' Frances retorted sharply. 'You'd look just as good as they do if you'd just take a little trouble. It is too bad, though, that there are so many more women than men. But that always seems to be the way.' She pointed at two tanned and muscular blond Adonises who were lounging at the side of the pool pretending not to notice the women. 'Those two, for example. They're the cocks of the walk, with all those hens competing for their attention.'

Melissa laughed. 'The women are all so attractive and sexy-looking that it must make it terribly hard for them to choose.'

Frances pursed her lips. 'You know, in spite of the common myth, men aren't all that interested in a voluptuous figure. I have two grown sons, and I know from experience that what draws men to women most of all is attention, appreciation.' She chuckled reminiscently. 'In fact, my own husband was very attractive to women, and, believe me, I was never anyone's idea of a sex symbol. It's character a real man is looking for, and a loving heart.'

'I'm sure you're right, Frances,' Melissa said with a smile. 'But the problem for people like me is meeting them.' She shook her head. 'I don't know what it is. Somehow I just freeze up in social situations where other women sparkle.'

Frances picked up her knitting again. 'Well, while it's true that character counts most of all, that doesn't mean you can't put a little icing on the cake.' Her mild blue eyes twinkled as she darted Melissa a quick glance, sweeping over her from head to toe. 'You are a little too thin, but you have a nice figure. In fact, some men find a slender build like yours quite sexy. Your skin is lovely, you have all that thick, dark, shiny hair, and with the right clothes you could be as attractive as the next girl.'

'You might be right,' Melissa murmured.

In fact, she knew Frances was right, at least about the clothes. Too bad she'd run out of money before she could buy the new wardrobe she'd had in mind. Except for *the* dress. By the time she'd paid for the cruise and bought the bare essentials, there had only been enough left for one really good item.

She'd decided on the sea-green party dress, just the colour of her eyes, the saleswoman had said. Now all she had to do was work up the courage to wear it. It was very revealing, and there wasn't that much of Melissa to reveal.

Frances reached out and laid a hand on her arm. 'Well, I hope you don't think you have to stick with me just to be polite. I do enjoy your company, but I can manage quite well on my own.'

'Oh, no, it's not that at all,' Melissa said hurriedly. 'I like talking to you. I'd just as soon watch the others as try to join them.' She gave a dry little laugh. 'And I'm definitely not interested in competing for those two men.'

Frances gave her a sharp look. 'Oh? You must have a young man of your own at home, then?'

Melissa looked away. 'No,' she murmured. 'Not now, I don't.'

Not for worlds was she going to discuss that subject with anyone, not even Frances. Even though the affair with Larry Conroy had ended bitterly over a year ago, the hurt still ran too deep to talk about with a virtual stranger, no matter how sympathetic.

Frances continued to stare at her for a moment or two, but when it was clear to her that Melissa intended to remain firmly silent she raised a hand to shield her eyes from the burning sun and shifted her gaze to the group around the pool.

'Well, I've got my money on that little redhead,' she remarked chattily. 'She's by far the prettiest of the bunch. I'll bet anything she walks off with one of them.'

While the older woman rambled on, Melissa relaxed and settled back in her chair, listening with half an ear. It was one of the things she liked best about Frances. The gossipy line of chatter was never malicious, and Melissa didn't have to think of things to say or try to entertain her in any way.

She was half asleep when she felt Frances jab her sharply in the arm with her elbow. 'Now, there's an interesting-looking man.' She spoke in a voice meant to be low, but which carried resonantly across the water. 'That one just coming out on deck. I've noticed he's as antisocial as you are.'

Melissa turned her gaze towards the stairs, where a tall man wearing dark trousers and a white cotton shirt was standing quite still. He seemed to be surveying the entire scene before him from behind his dark glasses, and from the rather frowning look of concentration on his lean, tanned face wasn't at all pleased with what he saw.

From that very first glimpse of him, there was something about the silent figure, an air of command in the arrogant lift of his dark head, the confident stance, that held Melissa, an odd shock of recognition. As she gazed at him, spellbound, little shivers began to run up and down her bare arms, as though the bright sun had gone behind a cloud. She could almost have sworn she knew him.

'Who is he?' she murmured to Frances, without taking her eyes off him for a moment.

'I have no idea,' Frances replied. 'But there's something about him, don't you agree?'

Melissa nodded. 'Yes.'

After a few moments of his silent scrutiny, the man began to stroll around the deck in long, deliberate strides, his hands clasped behind his back, his eyes fixed straight in front of him. As he went around the far end of the swimming-pool, there was a slight hush in the raucous babble, as though the noisy crowd there too had recognised a presence in their midst. Then it started up again as soon as he had passed by.

Frances gave a low chuckle. 'Did you notice how every female head turned to look at him as he passed by? A man like that one makes those two young hunks look like callow boys.'

Melissa smiled. 'Yes, I did notice that. But he didn't seem to. He just walked right on by as though they didn't exist.'

'He's somewhat of a mystery man, isn't he?' Frances went on when he disappeared from view around the mid-structure of the deck. 'He never speaks to anyone and hasn't even shown up for one meal in the dining-room.'

'Perhaps he isn't well,' Melissa said. 'Or it could be he's just shy.'

Although she was convinced from the man's whole bearing that this couldn't be true, it was an explanation she could relate to only too well. All her life she'd been cursed with a timidity that other people always misconstrued as a cold reserve, but which in reality was the bane of her existence. Somehow she'd hoped that plunging into a luxury cruise, spending all the bonus money they'd paid her as compensation for losing her job, would alter this state of affairs.

Instead, it had just pointed it up. It was one thing to have a reputation for stand-offishness in an office where she was well-known and her work appreciated, but quite another to be faced with yet another social situation where she was totally at a loss. She didn't even know how to begin to break into the laughing, carefree group around the pool.

'I don't think he's shy at all,' Frances went on. 'He has a touch-me-not, prickly look about him that simply screams "hands off".'

'Well, Frances, I know from experience how shyness can be misinterpreted that way. I've been accused of it many times myself.'

'Oh, no, dear, I'd never make that mistake about you. You're just timid, need to come out of your shell. That man has erected barriers. Believe me, I can tell. My son David is the same way.' She went on then to catalogue David's pecadilloes, and once again Melissa settled back into her own thoughts.

She dreaded having to look for another job when the cruise was over and she went back home to Santa

Barbara. She'd quite enjoyed the past two years working as secretary-receptionist and general dog's-body for the small struggling publishing firm. She'd seen the end coming for some months, so wasn't surprised when they'd told her they were closing up shop.

They'd been generous, given her the fat bonus that allowed her to take this cruise. Seven days of glamorous fun, the brochure had read, with organised activities, the opportunity to meet new people, bask in the sunshine, play on the beaches and explore the various stops along the way—places with exotic names like Puerto Vallarta, Manzanillo, Acapulco, Mazatlán.

So far she hadn't seen a sign of an organised activity, and the few places they'd stopped at hadn't been the picturesque villages she'd imagined, but only miles of white beach entirely lined with ultra-modern hotels and condominiums.

Frances was tidying up her knitting and preparing to leave. 'Well, my dear,' she said, rising up stiffly, 'I've had enough sun and fun for one morning. I have some letters to write before lunch. I'll see you later in the dining-room.'

When she was gone, Melissa lay back in her chair and watched the activity around the pool. Frances had certainly been right about the two golden boys. Their lazy eyes surveyed the women with identical haughty expressions, as though mentally plotting which to favour with their attentions. Frances had bet on the small redhead, and Melissa played a little game with herself, trying to calculate whom the other winner would be.

Whichever it was, Melissa didn't envy her. Those two men reminded her so much of Larry that it was almost funny, the same good looks and insouciant charm, and the same emptiness underneath.

Just then a bright red ball came whizzing through the air straight towards her. She could see it coming, but didn't have time to duck, and it hit her square in the middle of her forehead then landed in her lap. Although it startled her and knocked her slightly off balance, it was very light and did no damage.

With a laugh, she stood up to toss the ball back to the red-headed young woman, who was rushing over, her face stricken. She caught the ball, but kept on coming.

'Oh, I'm so sorry,' she said. 'Did it hurt you?'

'Not at all,' Melissa said with a smile. 'No harm done.'

'Well, that's all right, then,' the redhead said. She turned to go, but after a moment's hesitation turned back. 'Say, why don't you join us?'

Pleased, but a little flustered by the unexpected invitation, Melissa hesitated. Then she thought, Why not? It's the reason she'd come on the trip, after all.

'Why, yes,' she replied. 'I'd like that.' She set down her book and took off her towelling robe to reveal a modest one-piece bathing suit underneath.

'My name is Terry,' the redhead said as they walked together towards the pool.

'I'm Melissa.'

'Well, it's nice to know you, Melissa. Come on, I'll introduce you to the others.'

When the group broke up to dress for lunch, two hours later, Melissa retrieved her robe and book, then headed towards her stateroom on the deck below with a much lighter heart than she'd started out with that morning.

She had been accepted! She'd been part of the group! They knew her name! She'd even managed to talk a little.

Just as she reached the head of the stairs she heard Terry call after her. 'See you at lunch, Melissa. Why don't you join us at our table?'

Before she could answer, the redhead had turned back to her friend and walked away. Melissa stood there for a few moments, debating. She'd formed the habit of taking her meals with Frances, who had come to depend on it, she knew. But she'd understand. Wouldn't she?

She started slowly down the stairs, still so absorbed in her inner debate that she miscalculated her footing in the backless sandals she was wearing. Before she could stop herself, she began to fall, and would have plunged headlong down the steep metal steps if she hadn't bumped into a tall figure directly in her path.

'Oh!' she cried, as a pair of strong hands braced her by the shoulders. She looked up to find herself gazing directly at the mystery man who had been prowling the deck by himself earlier. He had removed his dark glasses, and his eyes were a cold slaty grey.

Her heart began to flutter wildly, her knees grew weak, and she put a hand shakily to her throat. The steely eyes continued to hold hers, as though he was able to see into the most hidden recesses of her soul. She felt powerless under that steady gaze, that firm grip, and as limp as a rag doll. If he'd suddenly started shaking her, she wouldn't have been at all surprised.

Finally he released her and moved back slightly. 'You should be more careful, young lady,' he said in a deep, stern voice. 'You could have given us both a nasty fall.'

'I—I'm sorry,' she stammered, still breathless from the narrow escape. 'I'm afraid I wasn't watching where I was going.'

'Obviously,' was the dry reply. Then he gave her a thin smile. 'I might not be around to rescue you next time.' He glanced down at the book she was carrying. 'I've noticed that you're a great reader. That's the new John le Carré, I see. He's one of my favourites, too.' He gestured towards the swimming-pool, where a few stragglers were still lingering. 'Now that you've joined the fun and games around the pool, I hope it doesn't mean you're going to give it up entirely.'

She opened her mouth, but before she could get a word out he'd nodded his dark head, swivelled on his heel and was continuing on his way.

She stood there for a moment staring after him, then started slowly down the stairs again. What in the world...? she wondered. Why should he care what she did? It was none of his business. Still, in spite of the rude tone, his words warmed her strangely. He seemed so absorbed in his own thoughts, and so determined to avoid all human contact, that it was surprising—and rather flattering—that he even knew she existed, much less how she spent her time.

While she dressed for lunch, the inner ongoing debate about whether to sit with Frances, as usual, or her new friends raged on. She knew what she *wanted* to do. No question. By sheer luck—or Terry's kind heart—she'd managed to be included in a group of young people her own age. How could she give that up now?

However, the remarks of that strange man kept intruding, and she couldn't help wondering what he would think if she abandoned Frances. But that was silly! She didn't even know him. And he certainly didn't know her. She'd do what she pleased.

She took one last glance at her reflection in the mirror before she left. The hours of physical activity in the sunshine had made a vast improvement. Her skin had a healthy pinkish tinge, her eyes sparkled, even her hair seemed to shine more brightly.

As it turned out, her inner debate had been so much wasted energy. When she entered the dining-room and saw Frances sitting there at their usual table, an expectant look on her face, she simply couldn't let her down. She could only hope the others would understand, and that it didn't spoil their acceptance of her.

'Well,' Frances said when she'd sat down, 'you look very perky. I noticed that you were playing with the young people this morning. Good for you.'

'Yes, it was fun. They're really quite nice when you get to know them.'

Frances leaned across the table. 'Listen, Melissa, there's no need for you to tie yourself to a boring old woman on this trip. I'll understand perfectly if you want to join them at meals from now on. After all, it's not written in stone that we eat together, just because we started out that way.'

'No,' Melissa replied hurriedly. 'But thank you for the thought. I do enjoy their company, but that doesn't mean I have to be with them every minute. It's probably just as well not to.'

'Well, you suit yourself. I just want you to know that you're perfectly free to do what you please.'

'Thanks, Frances. I appreciate that.'

Frances bent over closer again and gave her a triumphant grin. 'I found out who our mystery man is.'

'Really? How did you do that?'

'Oh, I have my sources.' She lowered her voice to a sibilant hiss. 'His name is Miles Thatcher.'

Melissa's eyes widened. 'Not *the* Miles Thatcher.'

Frances nodded with satisfaction. 'The very one. In fact,' she went on, leaning closer, 'he's here right now, back against the far wall. Finally decided to come and eat with the rest of us.'

Melissa glanced furtively behind her. Sure enough, there he was, sitting alone, the familiar dark head bent over the thick book propped up in front of him. Everything about him, from the closed-in look on his face to the hunched shoulders, virtually shouted 'Do not disturb'.

'But he's a famous writer. What's he doing on this cruise?'

Frances shrugged. 'Who knows? Actually, he's travelling incognito. The name on the passenger list is John Smith. Can you imagine trying to fool anyone with a phoney name like that? You'd think a writer would have more imagination. Apparently he goes on cruises periodically just to get away from civilisation. You know, the telephone, things like that.'

Melissa gazed at her friend in frank wonderment. 'Frances, how in the world did you find out all these things?'

Frances winked at her. 'Well, it helps to make friends with the purser. I've travelled on this ship before, and we're old pals.' She leaned forward again. 'He's quite a good-looking man, don't you think? I'll bet all those girls would love a chance at him, especially if they knew who he was, but I promised the purser I wouldn't breathe a word.' She lowered her voice to a dramatic hush. 'Rumour has it that before he wrote his first book he was involved in secret work for the government. You know, very hush-hush—and dangerous.'

Melissa widened her eyes. 'You mean he was a spy?'

'Oh, I don't know about that. Apparently he was a freelance journalist who just happened to be in the right place at the right time. You know. Vietnam, Cambodia. Some place like that.'

As Frances prattled on all through lunch with her titbits of inside information gleaned from her friend, the purser, Melissa listened with only half an ear. Miles Thatcher! A great reader, she had long admired his work. He wrote very intricate, very literate spy stories that were extremely popular, as well as critically acclaimed, he was one of the most famous writers in the world, and here he was, on the same ship as she was!

Then her cheeks began to burn at the memory of their brief encounter on the stairs that morning. She'd almost knocked down Miles Thatcher! Now his comments about her new friends seemed even more puzzling.

Just then, she heard a flurry of activity at the far end of the dining-room, voices raised, laughter. She looked up to see that very group coming towards her, apparently just leaving. When they passed by, she caught Terry's eye, and the small redhead smiled.

'We'll be putting in at Puerto Vallarta soon,' she called out. 'And we're all going ashore. Why don't you come with us?'

Melissa beamed. 'Why, yes,' she said. 'I'd like that.'

'Good. Meet you on deck in about an hour.'

With another little wave, Terry hurried after the group now straggling out into the corridor. Still smiling, Melissa turned to Frances, who was giving her a long, appraising look.

'Well,' she said. 'Sounds as though you've joined the young people after all.'

'Yes, isn't it great?' Then her face grew troubled. 'Oh, Frances, were you planning on my going with you?'

Frances threw up her hands and laughed heartily. 'Heavens, no! My poor feet would never keep up with you.' She reached across the table and put her hand over Melissa's. 'You go on ahead and have a good time. I'm just pleased you've made some proper friends.'

'Well, if you're sure...'

'Positive.' She wiped her mouth and set her napkin down on the table. 'Now, it's time for my nap. Have you finished?'

'Yes, and I'd better go get ready for the trip ashore.'

Suddenly Frances's mouth fell open and her eyes started to gleam as they shifted past Melissa to gaze fixedly at a point just beyond her shoulder. Puzzled, Melissa looked around to see Miles Thatcher striding towards them, apparently on his way out of the dining-room, his head down, his hands stuck in the pockets of his dark trousers, his book tucked under his arm.

She glanced back at Frances, who was slowly rising to her feet now, still staring, a very determined look on her face. Oh, no, Melissa thought in a sudden panic. She wouldn't! But she did. The minute he reached their table, Frances stepped out into his path so that he had to come to an abrupt halt.

'Oh, Mr Thatcher,' she said in a low voice. 'I hate to bother you, but I just had to tell you how much I admire your books, and could I please have your autograph?'

He simply stood there staring down at her for a moment or two, and as Melissa watched, mortified, the look of sudden shock on his face slowly hardened into a frown of annoyance. She knew he was going to refuse, and Frances would be crushed. She was already cowering back from him, as though afraid he might actually hit her.

Although she was annoyed at Frances for intruding on the man's privacy, when she saw the stricken look on her face, brick-red with embarrassment, Melissa felt a rush of sympathy for her. She meant no harm, and it wouldn't hurt him to give her the blasted autograph. What was more, someone should tell him so.

Melissa raised her chin and plunged into the icy waters. 'Mr Thatcher, I can understand and sympathise with your desire for privacy, but we mean you no harm.'

He turned to her, one heavy dark eyebrow raised, but remained silent. Well, at least he hadn't snapped her head off.

She took a deep breath. 'You're a famous man,' she went on haltingly. 'Shouldn't you expect to have to pay something for that fame?'

For a few fraught seconds he merely stood there gazing down his nose at her, the grey eyes narrowed, a little pulse beating along the bony jaw just below his ear. It was a tense moment, and Melissa steeled herself, waiting for the full blast of his wrath to descend on her. Anyway, she thought philosophically, he can't kill me. At least not here in front of all these people.

Then he wrinkled his forehead, as though working out
a puzzle. He cocked his head to one side and to her astonishment a faint flicker of an amused smile began to
twitch on the thin mouth, softening the hard features.
Slowly, his eyes never leaving hers, he reached into the
pocket of his shirt and pulled out a small notebook and
pen. He braced it on his book, flipped over several pages,
then turned to Frances.

'You'll have to tell me what name,' he said politely.

Frances beamed up at him. 'Oh, yes. It's Frances.
Frances Venable. And this is my friend, Melissa Ryder,'
she added.

Without another word, he scribbled on a page of the
notebook, ripped it out and handed it to her. 'Here,' he
said. 'And I would greatly appreciate it if you will keep
my identity quiet.'

Frances took it from him and held it up proudly, as
though it were made of solid gold. 'Oh, thank you,' she
burbled. 'Thank you so much. I do apologise for intruding on your privacy, and I promise I won't breathe
a word.'

Melissa glanced over at the sheet of paper. There, in
a slashing black script, she read, 'To Frances Venable.
Regards, Miles Thatcher.'

He had just turned to go, when Frances spoke up
again. 'Oh, Mr Thatcher,' she began, then, in a flurry,
amended it. 'I mean, Mr Smith. I wonder, could I per-
suade you to take an after-luncheon cup of coffee with
us?'

When Melissa saw his face close down again, she
groaned inwardly. Trust Frances to go that one step too

far. 'Oh, Frances,' she said quickly. 'I'm sure Mr Smith has more important things to do with his time.'

But when she darted him a quick apologetic look, she saw that the silvery eyes were alight with amusement. 'That's very kind of you,' he said. 'I'd like that.'

They sat back down at the table and ordered coffee from a nearby waiter, who didn't seem overjoyed at this prolongation of the lunch-hour. After he'd served them with a decidedly injured air, Frances leaned across the table and fixed Miles Thatcher with an admiring look.

'I must tell you,' she said in a low, hushed voice, 'how very much I have enjoyed your books. It must be wonderful to be able to create something out of nothing that way. A great satisfaction to you, I'm sure, not only the work itself, but the fame you've gained.'

He looked mildly surprised, as though he hadn't expected such insight from her. 'Why, yes,' he agreed. 'It is, in a way.' He gave a dry laugh. 'Although it does have its disadvantages. It's a nuisance to have to hide behind false names when I travel.'

Frances gave him an indulgent smile. 'Well, we're all naturally curious about famous people. It's a compliment, in a way.'

'Oh, yes. I realise that. And I wouldn't mind it so much if it were the books or the writing people were interested in. I've never refused to discuss those things. It's when reporters and other media interviewers try to dig into my private life that I balk.'

'Yes,' Frances murmured. 'I can understand that.' She hesitated for a moment, then leaned across the table and lowered her voice confidentially. 'You must be referring to your secret government work.'

He gave her a distant smile. 'Not really,' he replied
easily. 'Most of that is what the Press has manufactured. But tell me a little bit about yourself. Do you have
a family?'

He'd said the magic word, and, once launched on her
favourite topic, for the next half-hour Frances chattered
happily about her sons, their wives and children, her
dead husband, prompted every now and then by Miles
Thatcher whenever she showed signs of flagging.

During the entire time, Melissa sat silently by, sipping
her coffee and listening to the two of them chatting. She
couldn't help speculating about the private life he
guarded so jealously, and her imagination ran riot as she
pictured an exciting round of brilliant social affairs,
famous names, glamorous women.

Occasionally she sensed his eyes turn in her direction
and always hastily looked away when he did. She knew
he must be wondering why she was so tongue-tied and
cursed the shyness that kept her from taking advantage
of his company.

He was unlike anyone she'd ever met before, and she
was simply bowled over by the force of the man's personality, as well as deeply envious of Frances's ease, especially with such a larger-than-life figure. When Frances
spoke, he listened to her as carefully as though he considered her an important person in her own right instead
of merely an avid—and intrusive—fan.

Yet, when he'd drained his coffee, he rose so abruptly
to his feet that it was clear he was also the kind of man
who was used to doing exactly what he pleased, and had
no intention of staying one moment longer than *he* considered suitable.

'Thank you for the coffee, Mrs Venable,' he said politely. He turned to Melissa, gave her a brief nod, then turned and walked off in his customary gait, shoulders hunched slightly, hands stuck in his trousers pockets, his step unhurried, but quite determined.

'My!' Frances breathed the moment he was out of earshot. 'What a nice man!'

Melissa stared at her. 'Nice?' Then she laughed. 'Courteous perhaps, even tolerant. But I'd never call him nice.'

'Well, he was nice to me,' Frances replied stoutly. She gave her precious autograph one last glance before tucking it into her handbag. 'And that was certainly one of the most interesting conversations I've ever had in my life.' She gave Melissa a chiding look. 'But why didn't you join in?' She shook a finger at her. 'And don't try to tell me it was shyness. After all, you were the one who bearded the lion in his den and got the autograph.'

'Oh, that's different,' Melissa replied with a smile. 'I don't have a problem speaking my piece when there's a principle involved that's important to me.' She sighed and got up from the table. 'It's that dreadful small talk that ties my tongue in knots.'

Frances gave her a long, appraising look. 'Actually,' she said slowly, 'those looks he kept giving you weren't exactly critical.' She laughed. 'In fact, it could be that, compared to an old natterer like me, he was probably just admiring your quiet ways.'

CHAPTER TWO

IT DIDN'T take long that afternoon for Melissa to realise that the crowd she'd gone ashore with had no intention of doing any sightseeing. After a cursory jaunt along the main street, they headed straight for an air-conditioned cocktail lounge, settling in around a large table as though they intended to spend the entire day there.

It was exactly the kind of situation which made her most uncomfortable, consisting entirely of inconsequential chatter, meaningless small talk, for which she had no talent whatsoever, and a lot of sexual byplay between the two blond Adonises and the four other women present.

She sat there for as long as she could, smiling fixedly until her muscles ached, trying to act interested in the conversation, nursing an unfamiliar drink, full of fruit and much stronger than she was used to, until she couldn't stand it another moment longer.

She leaned over to speak to Terry, who was sitting next to her, and said in a low voice, 'If you don't mind, I think I'll go outside and stretch my legs for a while.'

'Sure, honey,' Terry said. 'We'll catch up with you later.'

Melissa pushed back her chair and, smiling apologetically at the others around the table, turned to go. As far as she could see, no one paid her the slightest attention, and she started towards the entrance with a feeling of deep relief.

Before she reached the door, however, she heard someone call her name. She looked around to see one of the blond young men coming after her. She stopped, puzzled. She had no idea he even knew her name, and she searched her mind for his. Jack, that was it.

'Melissa,' he said when he reached her side. 'I think I'll come too, if it's all right with you. I could use some exercise.' He gave her a dazzling smile, full of even white teeth that flashed in his deeply tanned face. 'Three margaritas in a row is all I can handle, and I need to walk them off before the cocktail hour begins.'

Although it surprised her that he had sought her out this way, it was also rather flattering. She'd worn her best cotton sundress that day, not new, but a nice shade of green, her best colour, and a perfect fit from several seasons of wear. It suited her slim figure, with a low square neckline and thin straps, and a woman with more voluptuous attributes couldn't have worn it nearly as well.

'Sure, Jack,' she said. 'I'd like the company.'

It wasn't until they were outside walking along the crowded street that she realised he hadn't been kidding about too many margaritas. Although he wasn't actually staggering, he did rather lurch along beside her, his eyes glazed and fixed straight ahead.

They'd only gone a few blocks when he suddenly stopped short and gave her an agonised look. 'I've got to find a place to sit down in the shade,' he muttered.

His face was ashen under his heavy tan, the bright blue eyes glazed over. He's going to be sick, she thought in a panic, right here in the middle of the main thoroughfare.

'I think there's a park just ahead,' she said quickly.

'Come on, then,' he said, taking her by the arm.

She almost had to run to keep up with him as he ploughed his way forward, heedless of the other tourists that thronged the pavement, bumping into them when they were in his way as though he owned the street. He was pulling her along so fast she hardly had a chance to take in the beauty of the small town, the sparkling blue bay, the stretch of white sand surrounding it, their ship tied up at the dock.

Clearly, however, his condition was desperate, and she managed to keep up with him until they came to a wide plaza with paved walkways winding among the trees. It too was full of tourists, and Jack pursued his same zigzag course through them.

Beyond the plaza they entered a small park. Jack made his way to a bench beside the paved path and flopped down heavily. With a sigh, he leaned his head back and closed his eyes.

Melissa stood looking down at him dubiously. Whatever had ailed him, he seemed to have it under control. At least he wasn't going to be sick in public.

No doubt about it, he was a very handsome man, with his bright shock of yellow hair, deeply tanned skin and regular features. In repose, however, his eyes closed, the muscles of his face slack, there was a weakness about his good looks, a softness about his rather pudgy cheeks that spoiled the impression of vibrant youth.

Why had he been so anxious to join her? On the ship and in the cocktail lounge he hadn't paid the least attention to her. Had he just wanted a nursemaid in case he did get sick? Or was she just an excuse to get away from his adoring admirers before he disgraced himself in front of them?

As the minutes ticked by and there was no sign of life from Jack, she glanced around the quiet park. The tall palm trees were swaying gently in the breeze that blew off the bay. From the plaza came the faint strains of a strolling mariachi band.

She looked down at Jack again. He had fallen into a deep sleep and was snoring softly. While she stood there debating what to do about him, she suddenly heard the sound of firmly measured footsteps heading her way, then stopping just behind her.

Startled, she turned around to see Miles Thatcher standing just a few feet off to one side, his arms crossed in front of him, looking down his nose at her, an amused smile creasing his lean face.

'Well, Melissa,' he said with a nod at Jack. 'I see your boyfriend has conked out on you.'

'I'm afraid so,' she replied, returning his smile. 'But he's not my boyfriend,' she added hastily.

He quirked one heavy black eyebrow and took a step towards her. 'Oh?' he said. 'I beg your pardon. I was sure you'd become the current favourite. For today, least.'

'Oh, no. We were all just having a drink. I wanted to do some sightseeing and Jack decided to come with me.' Why am I explaining all this to him? she wondered. It's none of his business what I do or whom I do it with.

He glanced down at the figure sprawled on the bench. 'Well, if sightseeing is what you had in mind, I'm afraid you're out of luck.'

The spark of humour in his voice took the sting out of his words, and she had to admit it really was rather funny. Jack's mouth was now hanging open, and the snores had escalated into a loud, sonorous sound that cut into the stillness like the roar of a train. In spite of herself, she began to giggle.

'Well,' she said, 'as a matter of fact I was just trying to decide whether it would be all right to leave him. It does look as though he's settled down for quite a while.'

'I would say,' he replied in a dry tone, 'that unless you've signed on as his keeper he can well take care of himself. I have no doubt that the bevy of adoring women will seek him out before long, and if you want my opinion I think you would be totally justified in going off on your own if that's what you want to do.'

'Well,' she said, 'if you really think he'll be all right.'

'I'm quite sure he will.' He nodded at her. 'Well, I'll be off now. Enjoy your afternoon.' He started to walk away then, but had only taken a few steps when he suddenly stopped and turned back to her. 'As a matter of fact,' he said slowly, 'I've rented a car for the afternoon and plan to take a drive down the coast, get away from all these damned hotels; you can join me, if you like. There are a couple of villages on the way that are quite interesting.'

Melissa was so dumbstruck at the unexpected invitation that she could only stare at him. Why? What could he possibly want with her? More to the point, did she want to go with him? For some reason she sensed danger in the man, as though the rather politely bland surface hid a volcano that could erupt at any moment.

'I don't know,' she said at last.

He gazed at her thoughtfully for a moment, then said in a light joking tone, 'What are you afraid of, Melissa? I'm not planning to abduct you, if that's what's worrying you.'

'No, of course not,' she replied, flustered. 'It's just that the others are expecting me to join them.'

He shrugged. 'Suit yourself. I just thought you might like to see something of the countryside. But if you prefer to stay with your friends, by all means do so.'

Just then the sound of loud shouting and high-pitched giggles broke the stillness. She looked up to see the others coming down the path towards them, and all of a sudden she knew she didn't want to spend the precious afternoon sitting in yet another darkened bar while all of sunny Mexico beckoned to her.

They hadn't seen her yet, and somehow she was certain that Miles Thatcher wouldn't want to be there when they arrived. She glanced at him. What harm could it do?

'Yes,' she said in a low voice. 'I'd like to go with you. But I'll have to tell them I'm leaving. Where's your car? I can meet you there.'

He pointed to the side-street on the other side of the park. 'I'm parked right over there. It's a grey Mercedes.'

'I'll just explain to them . . .' she began, but he had already turned and was striding away from her.

She turned to face the crowd, who had reached the bench by now, and were so caught up in making jokes at the sorry spectacle Jack made, still passed out on the bench, that they didn't pay any attention to her anyway. As soon as she could, she drew Terry aside.

'If you don't mind, Terry, I have some things to do, so I think I'll head off on my own now.'

'Oh, sure, honey,' Terry said. 'Suit yourself.' She laughed. 'Actually, with Jack out of commission one less female will be a blessing. You know, your walking off like that with one of the few men on board didn't win you any points with the other gals.'

'I'm sorry, Terry. It really wasn't my fault. I mean, I had no idea Jack meant to come with me.'

Terry raised her eyebrows. 'Listen, don't apologise. It's a jungle out there, every woman for herself.'

Melissa shuddered inwardly at the too-true analogy. 'Well, then, I'll probably see you back on board ship later.'

With a little wave, Terry turned from her and Melissa went off to find Miles Thatcher's car.

Although the long coastline was still dotted here and there with condominiums and hotels, they became less concentrated on the drive south. All along the way, Miles kept up a running commentary on the history, architecture and topography of the area. He seemed to like to expound, and since Melissa liked to listen it worked out quite well.

'Puerto Vallarta used to be a tiny fishing village, unspoiled and totally unknown to the outside world,' he explained. 'Then, in the Fifties, they made that damned film down here—*The Night of the Iguana*—and that was the end of paradise. Ever since, the tourists have been flocking down and all but wrecking the place.'

Even though it was true that the many new buildings were gradually encroaching on the pristine setting, Melissa was entranced by its beauty. Surrounding the enormous bay was mile after mile of beach, gleaming stretches of sand on one side of the road, the low foothills of the Sierra Madre on the other.

'It's still very beautiful,' she said. 'I thought Santa Barbara was lovely, but this beats anything I've ever seen.'

He gave her a swift sideways glance. 'Is that where you're from? Santa Barbara?'

'Yes. Born and raised there.'

'You're right. It is a lovely town. Of course it only stays that way because the city fathers wisely put a moratorium on industry right from the beginning.' He hesitated, then said casually, 'In fact, I have a place there myself.'

'Really? I had no idea.'

'No,' he stated flatly. 'Very few people do.' He flicked his eyes at her again. 'And that's the way I want to keep it.'

'I already told you,' she said, 'I won't give away your identity. Not here and not back home in Santa Barbara.'

'No, I don't believe you will.' He flashed a smile at her that totally transformed the hard features. 'I wouldn't have told you otherwise.' He turned his eyes back on the road. 'A writer learns to be a pretty fair judge of character.'

As they rode along, he went on to compare the scenery and atmosphere of Mexico to other places he'd been. Melissa found his picturesque descriptions fascinating. Obviously, he was a man who had travelled widely and enjoyed talking about the interesting things he'd seen. He had a low, well-modulated voice—a cultivated voice— and spoke in a crisp, self-assured manner.

'You've travelled a great deal, haven't you?' she asked during a lull. 'I mean, all those exotic places you've mentioned—Hong Kong, Singapore, Malaysia, India.'

'Yes, I suppose I have. I'm rather a restless soul, when it comes right down to it.'

'I envy you,' she sighed. 'I've never been anywhere.'

'Oh, you will,' he stated confidently. He turned briefly to give her another smile. 'You're very young, you know. You have your whole life ahead of you.'

'I'm twenty-seven,' she said defensively. 'That's not exactly a child.'

He threw back his head and laughed. 'Not to you, perhaps. Wait until you're almost forty. You'll change your mind. Now,' he said, sobering, 'I've done all the talking so far. Why don't you tell me something about yourself?'

Startled, she reddened. 'Oh, I'm not very interesting.'

'To a writer,' he stated firmly, 'every human being is interesting. I've never met a boring person.'

'Well, what do you want to know?'

'Do you have a job?'

She laughed wryly. 'I *did* have. I was a sort of secretary-receptionist in a small publishing house in Santa Barbara.'

'Sounds interesting. Right in my line, too. What happened?'

'They went bust,' she explained. 'In fact, the reason I could afford to come on this trip was because of the nice severance pay they gave me.'

He nodded. 'Too bad. What will you do now?'

She shrugged. 'I really haven't thought that far ahead. Look for another job, I suppose.'

'Do you have family to fall back on?'

'Afraid not. I'm an orphan.'

'I'm sorry.'

'Oh, don't be,' she said hurriedly. 'My parents died so long ago I'm quite used to looking after myself.'

'Yes,' he said softly. 'I can see that.'

They rode along in a soothing and pleasant silence for some time, with none of the embarrassing conversational lags that had tormented her in the past, when she'd spent agonising moments trying to think of something to say. He seemed so sure of himself, so in control of any situation that might arise, that it put her at ease.

From time to time she would sneak an occasional look at him as he drove. He was a hard one to figure out, one minute as prickly as a tiger defending his private territory, the next friendly and amusing. He drove well, in a relaxed manner, one armed braced on the open window, his hands lying lightly on the steering-wheel.

She wondered how old he was. With his dark glasses on, it was hard to tell from his eyes, but she did recall the crinkly lines at the corners, and a sort of ageless look of experience about them. He'd implied he was almost forty, but he didn't look it, especially when he smiled. Then he looked almost boyish. His face was long and lean, his features sharply etched, with deep lines running from his nose to his thin mouth, his dark hair thick and cut rather long.

They stopped for petrol in the tiny village of Tomatlan, a few miles inland from the coast. While the cheerful young Mexican boy filled the tank, Melissa and Miles drank a Coke under the shade of a gnarled live oak. He was leaning back against the trunk, while she stood some distance away from him, gazing out at the water, still visible from the rise they stood on.

'It's so peaceful here,' she said, turning back to him. 'I can see why you prefer it to the busier towns.'

He nodded. 'I love Mexico. In fact, I've been thinking about acquiring some property down here and building a place of my own. Nothing elaborate, just the bare necessities. I need to get away every once in a while.' He smiled at her. 'Solitude feeds the creative juices, and it's very hard to come by once you attain a certain amount of notoriety.'

She turned back to gaze out at the peaceful blue sea, drinking in the lovely view and wondering why he'd asked her along today if he wanted to be left alone.

After a moment, she heard him coming up behind her. Although he stopped just short of touching her, she could sense his strangely disturbing presence in every fibre of her being.

'If you're wondering why I invited you to come with me today,' he said softly, 'I can only tell you that I find you a curiously restful person.'

She swivelled her head around and goggled at him, astounded at his uncanny ability to read her very thoughts. 'You d-do?' she stammered.

'Oh, yes, little Melissa, I do indeed.' He reached out a hand to place it lightly on her cheek. 'There's something very refreshing about your innocence, your naïveté, something quite rare in the world I've lived in.'

She felt locked in the glittering grey gaze, softened now by a tenderness she wouldn't have dreamed existed in him. Then a wild thought came to her. Was this a pass? Was he going to kiss her? Did she want him to?

Just then the Mexican boy called out to them that the tank was filled, and Miles dropped his hand from her face.

'Come on,' he said. 'We should be heading back to the ship.'

The drive back was largely a silent one. Melissa was so confused by what had passed between them that she began to think it was all a dream. He sat beside her, his eyes hidden now behind his dark glasses, his expression inscrutable. Perhaps he was already regretting his display of tenderness.

When they arrived at the town, he dropped the car off at the rental agency, and they quickly walked the few short blocks to the dock, Melissa hurrying to keep up with his long strides.

'Thank you very much for the ride, Mr Thatcher,' she said a little breathlessly as they went. 'I really enjoyed it.'

'Miles will do,' he said shortly. 'And you're quite welcome.'

As they approached the ship, she noticed a small knot of men standing at the foot of the gangway, scanning the boarding passengers. Suddenly one caught sight of Miles and came rushing towards him, the others following close behind.

Miles stopped short, and Melissa heard him growl ominously deep in his throat. She gave him a quick look.

His face was like thunder, and he was glaring directly at her.

'So this is how you keep your word, is it?' he snarled.

Baffled at the accusing tone, she drew back and stared at him. A pulse was throbbing furiously at his temple, his mouth was set in a grim line, and he was obviously furious, holding himself in by main force, as though to keep from striking her.

'What—what do you mean?' she finally managed to stammer.

'Take another look,' he ground out with a toss of his head.

She turned quickly to see that the group of men were almost upon them by now, notebooks out, pencils poised and calling his name. Then she knew. And he clearly believed she was responsible.

'How can you think that?' she demanded hotly.

'What else *can* I think?'

'Well, all I can say is that I know I didn't tell anyone, and I can't believe Frances would either after she promised.'

'Then what's your explanation?'

'Well, Frances found out, didn't she?' She was growing just a little irritated herself by now. 'Someone had to tell her.'

But it was too late for explanations. The reporters were upon them now, blocking his way, hurling one question after another at him, not waiting for answers, interrupting each other.

Miles raised a hand. 'Just hold on a minute!' came his voice, loud, clear and commanding. There was immediate silence. 'Now,' he went on. 'If you please. I have exactly two minutes, and I'll answer one question at a time.'

While Miles dealt with them, Melissa slunk over to one side. She stood there watching for few seconds, then started walking slowly towards the ship. When she reached the gangway there came a great blast of the horn. She jumped, then scurried aboard.

She dressed for dinner that evening with special care. She was still a little hurt, even angry, that Miles had believed her capable of betraying his confidence, but she also felt sorry for him and could understand better now just why he guarded his privacy. Most of all she wanted a chance to convince him she was innocent.

Although her meagre wardrobe didn't offer much in the way of *haute couture*, still, the sun had brought out the gold streaks in her brown hair and she was pleased to see that she had a good enough tan by now to wear the rather nice white cotton dress that set it off so well. She also took special care with her make-up, applying a soft coral lipgloss and just a trace of emerald eye-shadow to highlight the green in her hazel eyes.

It was still light out as she climbed the metal stairway up to the dining-room, and she stood for a moment at the deck, gazing out towards the sea, calm now in the early evening, like a flat deep blue carpet spread out before her, until it dwindled away into the far horizon. The sun was sinking low, spreading a wide golden swath across the water, and the sky was a riot of brilliant shades of red.

The first gong rang for dinner just then, and she turned abruptly, almost bumping into Jack, who had come up silently behind her. Startled, she backed away from him a step.

'Jack!' she said. 'I didn't hear you!'

'Sorry,' he said, with a rather sheepish grin. 'I didn't mean to scare you.'

'Oh, that's all right. I was just standing here day-dreaming.' She waved a hand towards the sea. 'It's such a beautiful sight.'

She gazed at him, waiting, wondering what he wanted with her. He looked quite handsome in a loose full white shirt and skin-tight dark trousers, his blond hair sleeked back, his ruddy complexion glowing from a recent shave, his white teeth flashing against the deep tan of his face when he smiled. Yet in spite of his confident air there was something hangdog in his whole manner, and his blue eyes were decidedly bloodshot.

'I—uh——' he began haltingly, staring down at the deck. Then he raised his eyes. 'I want to apologise for conking out on you this afternoon.' He shrugged. 'Too many margaritas, I'm afraid.'

'Oh, don't give it another thought,' she assured him hastily. 'It could happen to anybody. How are you feeling?'

'Much better. Better than I deserve anyway.' He paused for a moment. 'Uh—are you going in to dinner now?'

She nodded. 'Yes, and I'm starved. How about you?'

'I'm not sure,' he replied with a frown. 'I'll let you know after I've given it a try. Hope it's not one of those spicy Mexican dishes. I don't think I'm quite up to that.'

She laughed and started moving away towards the dining-room. 'Well, there's always bread and butter, I guess.'

To her surprise, he turned and fell into step beside her. 'How about having dinner at our table tonight?' he asked gruffly. 'You know, the same crowd.' He grinned boyishly. 'I'd like to prove to you I can get through an evening sober.'

They had reached the doorway to the dining-room, and Melissa glanced inside, swiftly scanning the room for Miles. There was no sign of him, but she did see Frances sitting at their usual table alone, obviously waiting for her.

She turned to Jack. 'I'm sorry, Jack. I always eat with Frances, and I see she's there already.'

Puzzled, Jack looked past her. 'That old gal?' he asked incredulously. 'How did you get stuck with her?'

Melissa bristled. 'I'm not "stuck" with her at all,' she said stiffly. 'I like her very much.'

'Well, she won't mind if you eat with us, will she?'

'Probably not. But I feel an obligation to her. You don't do that to friends—leave them in the lurch just because you happen to feel like it.'

'Then you do feel like it? I mean, you're not turning me down because you're mad at me for the way I acted this afternoon?'

'No, of course not. I just think I should eat with Frances.'

'Well, maybe a dance and a drink at the disco later?' he asked hopefully.

'All right. I'd like that.'

As she made her way towards Frances, she had to wonder what had brought on Jack's sudden interest in her. She wasn't his type, he had every other woman on the ship angling for his attention, and he certainly knew by now she was no party girl. And maybe she'd been wrong to turn him down. Frances *would* understand, would even encourage her to mingle with the younger crowd.

Of course, a moment's reflection told her that she knew quite well why. She was still hoping Miles would show up. And even if he was still angry, she didn't want him to see her with Jack.

'Well, you look very nice tonight,' Frances said as Melissa took the chair across from her. 'That white dress just suits you, and you've acquired quite a nice tan.'

'Why, thank you, Frances.'

Frances glanced at the crowd of young people, now making their way towards their usual table. 'What was all that about?' she asked. 'Seems to me you have that blond Adonis eating out of your hand.' She leaned across the table and lowered her voice. 'Now, I've told you before, Melissa, that I want you to enjoy yourself with your own age-group. You mustn't feel tied to me.'

'Thanks, Frances,' she replied with a smile. 'But to tell you the truth I'm not so sure I really fit in with them.'

'Oh? I thought you went ashore with them after lunch today.'

'Well, I did, but it didn't work out very well.' She told her about the boring hours she'd spent in the cocktail lounge and how Jack had followed her, then passed out cold on the park bench.

Frances laughed. 'And what did you do then?' she asked. 'I hope you didn't have to take care of him.'

'No. Luckily the others came and took him off my hands.'

'So, how did you spend your afternoon then? I didn't see you on deck, so I assumed you stayed ashore the whole day.'

Melissa hesitated. She could lie and say she'd just gone sightseeing or shopping on her own, or she could tell her the truth, that she'd spent the afternoon with Miles Thatcher.

'I'm sorry,' Frances said, obviously sensing her hesitation. 'I didn't mean to pry.' She opened the menu. 'Now, let's see what we're going to have for dinner.'

Melissa finally decided to let it drop. Frances didn't seem offended by her reticence, and there was no point in making any excuses or trying to explain. She picked up her own menu, but before looking at it she gave the room another quick survey.

Still, Miles Thatcher was nowhere in sight.

As it turned out, she never did get the chance to speak to him in the days that followed. She only saw him occasionally, prowling around the deck just as before, his hands clasped behind his back, scowling behind his dark glasses, never speaking to anyone, no one daring to speak to him.

In the meantime she was enjoying her new friends. Once the other women realised she had no designs on Jack, they welcomed her back into the fold, and although she still had all her meals with Frances the rest of her time was almost entirely taken up with them.

They swam in the pool every day, played shuffleboard and volleyball, then gathered in the disco every night after dinner for music and dancing. And whenever the ship docked at an interesting port she always went ashore with them.

Soon they were homeward-bound, the trip almost over, with only a few more days left. All in all, Melissa felt it had been a success, money well-spent. She'd acquired a nice tan, made new friends she hoped to keep, and enjoyed seeing Mexico. Yet the memory of that one afternoon she'd spent with Miles remained the high point of the whole trip.

The last leg of the voyage was spent cruising along the protected waters of the Gulf of California, between the Mexican mainland and the long peninsula of Baja California. The weather had held beautifully, but as they approached the Cape of San Lucas at the southern tip of the peninsula storm clouds began to gather in the darkening sky, and the water became rough and turbulent.

To Melissa's relief, she found she was an excellent sailor, even when the gentle rocking motion of the ship escalated alarmingly into a veritable see-saw. It was their last day out. Tomorrow they would dock at San Diego, and as she stood at the railing of the deck in the pouring rain, thrilled to the core at the sight of the gigantic waves that crashed against the sides, the rolling of the slate-grey ocean, her feelings were mixed. She'd had a lovely time, but now she was faced with reality, and the first thing she had to do was find a job.

A depressing thought, made even more so by the fact that tonight was the grand ball, the farewell party, and since almost all her friends were in their cabins, prostrate with seasickness, it looked as though she might be the only one able to attend, at least of her crowd. Even Frances had succumbed.

She turned around to gaze at the bleak sight of a deck totally devoid of any of the other passengers, the chairs fastened down, the pool empty, and decided she might as well go back to her cabin and read. She still had to pack, too.

Just then the tall, familiar figure of Miles Thatcher appeared at the top of the metal stairway. At the sight of him Melissa stopped short and caught her breath. It was the first time she'd seen him alone since their afternoon together. His head was bent, and he was bundled up in a waterproof jacket, the collar turned up, his hands in the pockets, his dark hair blowing in the wind.

Suddenly he raised his head and their eyes met. He stood stock-still for a moment, gazing at her, his face expressionless. Melissa wondered if he would simply ignore her. That would be difficult to do, since they were alone on the deck, but she had a feeling that wouldn't bother him. He'd do exactly as he pleased.

Then he came walking slowly over to her, stopping at the railing beside her. 'I see you're a better sailor than your friends,' he commented.

'Yes, I'm very lucky, I guess.'

He turned from her and bent over the railing, his arms braced on the top rung, looking out at the foaming waves for a few moments. Melissa watched him covertly. He looked tired, the little lines at the corners of his eyes deeply etched, the forehead furrowed.

He turned around and leaned back against the railing. 'I've been wanting to speak to you, Melissa, but you always seem to be surrounded by the others.' He hesitated a moment. 'I just wanted to tell you that I found out it was the purser who spilled the beans to those reporters after all.'

'Well, I'm glad to hear that.' She waited for some kind of apology, but when he did finally speak his tone was faintly mocking.

'With your friends all out of commission, how will you manage with no one to play with?'

Melissa frowned. 'I'm not sure I understand.'

He shrugged. 'Well, you've spent the last several days so taken up with fun and games, it must be quite a letdown for you to be thrown back on your own resources.'

The sarcastic tone ruffled her. 'There's nothing wrong with my resources,' she said stiffly.

He raised a heavy dark eyebrow. 'Oh? I must say, Melissa, I'm rather disappointed in you. I had you figured for a sensible girl who had better things to do with her time than fritter it away on pointless activities with a bunch of mindless cretins.'

She really bristled at that. Miles Thatcher or not, he had no right to criticise her or her friends. She pulled herself up to her full height and glowered at him darkly.

'They are not cretins,' she stated in a heated tone. 'They happen to be very pleasant people who are enjoying themselves on a holiday. Which is more than I can say for you.'

Both eyebrows shot up at that, then lowered into a forbidding scowl. 'And just what do you mean by that?' he asked.

'Well, after all, this *is* supposed to be a pleasure trip!' she said stoutly. 'Why did you even bother to come if the only fun you get out of it is hiding away in your cabin and passing judgement on everyone else?'

For a few long moments he simply stood there glaring down at her. She raised her chin, waiting for the scathing tirade she felt certain was coming. He was far too clever for her, but she'd had her say and she'd stick to it. Granted he might well be superior to other mere mortals in some respects, but that didn't give him the right to judge them—or her—simply for having a good time.

Finally, his features relaxed and to her amazement the corners of his mouth began to twitch. He was actually chuckling!

'All right,' he said. 'You probably have a point. I do tend to be somewhat over-critical at times. And I'm glad you've had a good trip.'

'Thank you,' she said stiffly, still not mollified.

'When I said I was disappointed in you,' he went on in a softer tone, 'what I really meant was that I believed there was more substance to you than in the others.' He chuckled again. 'Of course, the way you just put me in my place proves you have more spirit than people give you credit for.' He nodded. 'I like that.'

She didn't know how to respond to that, and before she could think of something he'd nodded again, turned on his heel, and was striding away from her down the rolling deck.

CHAPTER THREE

STORM or no storm, Melissa was determined to go to the farewell ball that night looking her best, even if it turned out she was the only one to show up. She'd spent a fortune on that green party dress, and by gum she was going to wear it.

Actually, by nine o'clock, when the party was to begin, the ship had rounded the cape and the weather had calmed considerably. Although there was still a gentle swell, the rocking motion was not nearly so pronounced as it had been during the day, and out on deck the black clouds in the night sky were slowly dispersing, a crescent moon intermittently visible behind them.

As she climbed the stairway she could hear the band playing, the sound of voices, and she felt a little thrill of anticipation. With a luck a few of the younger crowd might also have escaped the ravages of the rough sea and come to the party after all.

However, when she reached the entrance to the large ballroom it was virtually empty, and a crushing sense of disappointment filled her. The few hardy souls seated at the tables scattered around the edges of the dance-floor were mostly older couples she didn't know. Frances wasn't there, nor any of the younger crowd.

Nor was Miles Thatcher anywhere to be seen. And she knew then that ever since his near-apology that afternoon she'd unconsciously been nursing the hope that she'd see him one last time before the cruise ended and she had to face reality again.

Still, the room was decorated nicely with coloured lanterns and streamers, the music pleasant, and she'd just have to make the best of a bad situation. A scattering of white-jacketed waiters stood idly along the sidelines, watching the one elderly couple who had the courage to get out on the still gently swaying floor and dance. They at least seemed to be having a wonderful time.

One of the waiters came scurrying up to her, obviously thrilled to have something to do. 'A table for two, *madame*?' he asked hopefully.

She gave him a rueful smile. 'Sorry. For one, I'm afraid.'

With a sigh he turned and led her to one of the choicest tables, directly on the dance-floor. She knew he meant it as a kindness, but still she felt uncomfortable out there in plain sight, and would have preferred a less public spot.

She sat there alone, sipping on a glass of wine and watching the people dancing—or rather, trying to dance—to the lilting strains of the mariachi band. Gradually, as the evening wore on, a few more people straggled inside, even a few young married couples with their children in tow. They all looked decidedly pale, however, from the day's ordeal, and none of them stayed long.

By ten-thirty she was ready to give up. There was no point sitting there by herself when it was clear that no one she knew was going to show up. She took one last sip of wine, set the glass back on the table, still half-full, and had just risen to her feet when she saw Jack coming towards her.

She'd never been so glad to see anyone in her life. He was resplendent in a well-fitting dinner-jacket, and, although still a little green about the gills, was grinning broadly, one hand raised in greeting. As he came closer, she noticed that he wasn't exactly walking. It was more like weaving, and she wondered if it was from the motion of the ship—or something else.

When he reached the table she found out quickly enough the moment he leaned towards her, opened his mouth and a gust of alcohol-laden breath was wafted her way. At this point, however, she was so glad to see a familiar face that she couldn't have cared less what condition he was in.

'Well,' he said, taking a seat opposite her, 'it looks as though we're the only two who'll make it tonight.' He glanced around the near-deserted room. 'Pity. It could have been fun.'

'Yes, it's too bad we hit bad weather on the night of the big party,' she replied. 'But I'm glad to see you haven't been laid low like all the others.'

He rolled his eyes. 'Oh, I was. Believe me, I was. I've never been so sick in my life. But now that it's calmed down I think I just might live.' He grinned. 'And I never miss a party if I can help it. How about you?'

'I seem to have escaped. Just lucky, I guess.'

He beckoned to a passing waiter and ordered a rum and Coke, then turned to her with a deadpan expression. 'I've given up margaritas,' he explained, slurring his words.

She had to smile. He was incorrigible, hopeless, a pretty little boy who would never grow up. But he was someone to talk to, and she was grateful for his company.

When his drink arrived he took a long swallow, wiped his mouth with the back of his hand, and set the half-empty glass back on the table. 'Ah, that helps to settle my stomach,' he said.

'I'm sure it does,' she replied in a dry tone.

He finished his drink and held up his hand for another. 'How about you?' he asked.

She raised her wine glass. 'I'm fine with this for now.'

He seemed to be trying to focus more steadily on her, blinking in the dim light. When he finally managed it, the blue eyes flicked her up and down and he gave her a foolish grin.

'My, don't you look sexy tonight,' he said, his voice low and suggestive. 'I like that dress. What there is of it, that is.'

She flushed and took a quick sip of her wine. If even Jack, in his inebriated state, noticed the dress, she probably shouldn't have worn it—or bought it in the first place. She especially didn't want to give him ideas.

In her cabin, getting ready, it hadn't seemed so bad. Granted, the neckline plunged rather low and the bodice was held up by two thin straps that buttoned on to the bodice at the back and were virtually invisible, but with her slim figure she didn't think it looked too provocative, at least not nearly the way it might if she were endowed with more generous proportions in certain quarters.

Suddenly Jack let out a loud guffaw of a laugh. 'Ha!' he exclaimed. 'I've ruffled your feathers at last.' He leaned across the table, grinning at her. 'Don't be embarrassed. I like my women sexy. It's a compliment.'

Before she could think of a proper reply, Jack had pushed his chair back and was stumbling to his feet. 'Shall we dance?' he said, holding out a hand.

Gazing up at him, standing there weaving unsteadily back and forth, she wasn't sure that was such a good idea. 'I don't know, Jack,' she said dubiously. 'Do you really think you're up to it?'

'Of course I am!' he exclaimed loudly, waving his arm in the air. He held out a hand to her. 'Come on. We'll show these old fogies how to dance the rumba properly.'

Melissa had never danced the rumba in her life, and she didn't think for one minute Jack had, either, but what would be the harm in trying? In his condition, he'd no doubt tread all over her feet, possibly even fall down in the middle of the dance-floor, but she wanted to have at least one dance on the last night of the voyage, even if it was a joke.

Once out on the floor, he immediately put both arms around her, pulling her tightly up against him. She'd never danced that way—in fact had hardly danced at all since her school days—and didn't know quite what to do with her hands. She couldn't just let them hang by her sides. Finally, she placed them lightly on his shoulders, and away they went.

As he propelled her clumsily around the floor, his cheek pressed close to hers, his rum-laden breath pungent in the close air, she started to enjoy herself. Although he could be a royal pain, he was basically such a good-natured soul that it was hard to take offence at him. And she was grateful for his company.

When the piece ended, Jack left her in the middle of the floor and went to speak to the leader of the band. As he stumbled back to her they broke into a lively tango. Jack immediately grabbed her and began to swoop her around the floor in a pretty fair imitation of the real thing.

By the time it was over she was breathless, helpless with laughter at his antics. As a finale, he leaned over her, forcing her backwards until she was sure she'd fall. When the last resounding chord was still echoing, there came the sound of scattered applause.

Jack pulled her upright, and she glanced around to see that they were the only couple on the floor. All the others were standing in a circle around them, clapping exuberantly. There was even one shouted, 'Bravo' from the rear.

Melissa was embarrassed at being the centre of attention, but at the same time exhilarated. It was a heady sensation to be the star of the show for the first time in her life.

'Come on,' Jack was muttering in her ear. 'Take a bow.'

She gave him a startled glance. 'Oh, Jack, I couldn't.'

'Sure you could. Look, I'll show you.' He turned to the circle of admirers and performed a sweeping bow, still so unsteady on his feet that he almost toppled over. Melissa had to giggle at the comical sight, and, entering into the spirit of the occasion, she dropped a deep curtsy. There was a renewed burst of applause, which only died down when the band began to play, a slow tune this time.

Still glowing, she turned to Jack, who already had his arms out, reaching for her. 'That was fun,' she said. 'But exhausting. I think I'd better sit this one out.'

He nodded. 'OK. Let's take a stroll out on deck, check out the weather. It feels like it's pretty calm by now.'

'Yes,' she agreed. 'That sounds like a good idea.'

'I'll just go get my drink...' he began, but she took him by the hand and tugged at him.

'Oh, come on, Jack. It can wait for five minutes. I think at this point a breath of fresh air would do you more good than rum.'

Outside the clouds were completely gone by now. A million stars dotted the dark blue sky, and the bright moon was reflected in the water, which had settled down to a gentle lapping motion.

'Ah, this is the life,' Jack said, stretching his arms wide. 'God, how I hate to go back.'

'Yes. I know what you mean. Do you have a job to go to?'

He shrugged. 'If you can call it that. I'm an actor, trying to break into the film industry. The toughest job on earth.' He gave her a rueful glance. 'By day I'm a shoe salesman.'

'Well, there's nothing wrong with that. At least you have a job. I suppose it takes a lot of experience to become an actor.'

'Yes. The problem is getting the experience. Parts for budding actors are as scarce as hen's teeth in Hollywood.'

'Well, I'm sure you'll make a success of it one of these days. You're young, and you certainly have the looks for it. You'll just have to stick at it until you get a break.'

He gave her a long look. 'You know, you're quite a girl, Melissa.' He waved a hand in the air. 'All those others, they just want a passably good-looking guy as a sort of trophy. You seem to be interested in me just as a person.' He gave her a sheepish grin. 'Even though I seem to be half-tight every time we're together.'

It was true he was still feeling the effects of the rum concoction he'd been drinking, but the dance and the fresh air did seem to have sobered him somewhat. At least he wasn't weaving around or slurring his words quite so much.

Melissa laughed at his hangdog expression. 'Well, let's just say that when you're sober you're a very nice person.'

He was staring at her so fixedly now that she began to grow uncomfortable under that steady scrutiny, and to wonder what it might be leading to.

'Melissa,' he said at last.

'Yes?' she replied lightly.

He moved a step closer to her. 'You really do look sexy in that dress,' he said huskily, and reached out for her. 'I like you a lot, Melissa. And I think you like me, too.'

He was pulling her towards him now, and she wasn't quite sure what to do. While a kiss from a handsome man on a romantic moonlit night would make a nice ending to the trip, Jack wasn't really the man she wanted.

Before she could make up her mind, his mouth came down on hers in a very wet open-mouthed kiss, and his tongue pushed against her firmly closed lips. That wasn't exactly her idea of a tender interlude, and all she really felt was a mild distaste.

'Oh, baby,' he now breathed in her ear. 'What you do to me.'

His hands began to travel, over her hair, her face, her neck, her bare shoulders. She felt as though she was in the arms of an octopus, not a man, and when she felt the hand on her shoulder slide downward to fumble at her breast she pushed it firmly away.

'No, Jack,' she said.

'Oh, come on, don't be coy,' he muttered in her ear. 'Just relax and enjoy it. You know you want it as much as I do.'

She looked at him, swaying before her, leering at her, a knowing look in his bloodshot blue eyes, a slack smile on his handsome face. Why, he's only a boy, she suddenly realised, and a weak one at that.

'Sorry, Jack,' she said at last, pulling herself out of his embrace. 'That's not on.'

But before she could even guess what he had in mind or had time to stop him he had reached out and pulled down one flimsy strap of the green dress and was now trying to slide his hand underneath the bodice. Fun was fun, she thought in a sudden panic, but this was getting out of hand.

'I said no, Jack,' she stated firmly. 'And I meant it.'

She could have been talking to the sea. He was so intent on his exploration that she might not even have been there. He seemed determined to get underneath that bodice, and this time when he yanked at the strap it broke away from the tiny button that held it in place at the back.

Really annoyed by now, she stamped her foot and slapped the groping hand. 'Stop it, Jack!' she said firmly. 'I mean it.'

'No, you don't.'

'I think she does,' came a low voice from behind him.

Startled, Melissa looked to see Miles Thatcher standing just behind Jack. He was scowling darkly, his hand gripping Jack's shoulder. Jack turned around slowly to face him.

'And just who are you?' he mumbled.

'That doesn't matter,' Miles said. 'When a lady says no, a gentleman has to take her at her word. Now, I think it would be a good idea if you went inside.'

Obviously bewildered at the sudden intrusion, Jack looked at Melissa. 'Is that what you want?' he asked.

'Yes, Jack, I do. I've been trying to tell you that.'

He scratched his head. 'Well, if you're sure...' He gave Miles a pugnacious look. 'But it's because she wants me to, not because you're making me.'

'Right,' Miles replied equably. 'You're only being a gentleman.'

'Damn right,' Jack muttered.

He turned then and as he walked unsteadily away there came the sudden sound of high-pitched voices from inside the ballroom. Apparently his friends had shown up after all, and there would be plenty of young women eager to play games with him now.

Melissa looked at Miles. He had moved away from her as soon as Jack left, and was leaning back against the railing, his arms folded in front of him. He was dressed in evening clothes and made an elegant sight with his lean form silhouetted against the moonlit sky, the stiff white shirt brilliant against his tanned face. He was gazing at her through narrowed eyes, a severe expression on his face.

For some reason he appeared to be angry with her, and she gave him a tentative smile. 'Uh—thank you,' she said. 'For rescuing me, that is.'

He came walking towards her, his hands in his trousers pockets, jingling keys and change, and stood before her for a moment, looking down his nose at her, his thin mouth set in a severe line.

'Well,' he said at last. 'That was quite a spectacle.'

She stiffened. 'I don't know what you mean. Jack's not really a bad sort. He just had a little too much to drink.'

'That seems to be a habit of his,' was the curt response. 'I saw the way he was lurching around with you on the dance-floor.' Then he smiled, and the steely eyes glinted as they swept her up and down. 'You look as though you've just been through a major battle.'

It was then it dawned on her that the strap of her dress was still flapping loose. Hastily she grabbed it and held it in place.

'Well, I guess things did get a little out of hand.'

'I don't know what else you could expect in that outfit you have on,' he commented drily. 'Even someone as naïve and gullible as you seem to be should realise that flaunting yourself that way is bound to attract some unwanted attention.'

She raised her chin and met his gaze. 'I'm not *that* naïve,' she retorted. 'If Jack had been sober he would have behaved himself no matter how I was dressed. You can't blame me...'

'Hey, hold on,' he said, holding up a hand. 'I'm not the bad guy here, remember. I'm the knight in shining armour who came charging up on his white horse to rescue you, after all.'

She had to smile. 'Well, thank you again. Now I guess I'd better go to my cabin and try to repair the damage.'

'Turn around,' he said. 'Maybe there's something I can do. You don't want to leave the party just yet, not on the last night.'

She gave him a dubious look, but finally decided there could be no harm. 'All right,' she said. 'There should be a small button at the edge of the bodice—that is if Jack didn't tear it off.'

She turned around, waiting, and when she felt his fingers on her bare back, fumbling for the button, a little shiver went up and down her spine at the touch. His hands were warm, his fingers deft, and when they continued to linger there for some moments after he'd finished fastening the strap in place she felt gripped by some strange sensations. Her heart skipped a beat, then seemed to flip-flop erratically until it finally settled down to a steady thudding.

'There,' he said at last, dropping his hands. 'That was a simple operation.'

When she turned to face him again, he had stepped back a pace and was giving her an indulgent smile, something like a fond uncle who had just fastened a small niece's pinafore. For some reason, this irritated her.

'Thank you,' she said shortly. 'Now, aren't you going to pat me on the head and tell me to be a good girl and go out and play with the other children?'

He stared at her for a moment, obviously taken aback by the tart comment. Then he threw his head back and laughed. As she watched him, the long column of his neck, the elegant formal wear, the supreme confidence of the man, a little ache of longing she couldn't quite define began to tug at her heart.

'You know, Melissa,' he said, still laughing, 'you've got a sharp tongue for such a timid girl. It's no wonder you made a conquest of that loutish surfer where all the others have failed.' He gave her a long look. 'And I assume there's a young man at home in Santa Barbara breathlessly waiting for your return?'

'No,' she said slowly. 'Not really.' She raised her chin. 'And Jack isn't a lout.' Then she had to smile. 'Although I think you're probably right about the surfing.'

'And why isn't there a young man?' he persisted.

She gave him a wary look. 'Why do you ask?' she said. 'Does it matter?''

'No,' he replied with a shrug. 'I guess not. I'm just a very inquisitive type. But there has been someone, hasn't there? A boyfriend, a lover? Perhaps even a husband.'

'I haven't spent my entire life knitting by the fire, if that's what you mean,' she replied tartly.

'I thought so,' he said with a knowing smile. 'Someone important, too, wasn't it? For a girl like you it would have to be.'

'Well, yes, but it was a long time ago, and I don't like to talk about it.'

'Ah, like that, was it? Well, never mind. We've all had our knocks in the game of love.'

'Even you?' she asked.

He gave her a startled look, then laughed shortly. 'Well, I haven't lived like a monk, if that's what you mean. But I can't afford serious romantic complications in my life. My work is everything to me, and I decided long ago that I'd just have to avoid anything that might disturb it.'

'Does it necessarily follow that a serious involvement with a woman would harm your work? I mean, lots of dedicated men have been married, had families.'

'Perhaps. I have no quarrel with what other men do. I just know what's necessary for me.'

Although his tone was pleasant enough, there was a note of such finality in it that she knew the subject was closed. Yet she wasn't ready to leave him, not just yet. It was the last night out, the last time she'd ever see him. Nor did he seem especially anxious to go. In fact, from the way his fingers had lingered on her bare back when he'd fastened her strap...

Turning abruptly, she walked over to the railing and stood there gazing out at the calm sea, the moonlit sky, and listening to the gentle lap of the waves against the side of the ship, the sounds of music and laughter from the ballroom. It was pleasantly warm, and there was a pungent tang of salt water in the air.

In a moment he came up beside her and leaned over the railing, his elbows braced on the top rung. They stood there together in an easy silence for some time. Melissa was content just to be there with him. Since he'd stayed with her, he obviously had no objection to her company, even seemed to enjoy it. What had he said that day of their drive? He found it restful.

Finally he turned to her. 'Well, Melissa,' he said softly. 'Has your vacation been everything you hoped it would be?'

'Oh, yes,' she said. 'I've had a wonderful time. I just hate to see it end.'

'Have you decided what you're going to do about a job when you get back to Santa Barbara?'

'Not really.' She laughed. 'Actually, I haven't given it a thought. Now, though, I guess I'll have to come up with something.'

'Are you a good secretary?'

'Well, I think so. I mean, I'm an accurate typist, and although my shorthand is rusty from not using it for so long I can operate just about any kind of tape recorder or dictaphone. We had some pretty ancient equipment at my old office.'

'And, best of all,' he said quite soberly, 'you can keep your mouth shut. That's one of the most important qualifications for any secretary, in my view. Discretion.' He gave a rueful laugh. 'I had a secretary once who confided the plot of my current book—not to mention some rather interesting details of my personal life—to a boyfriend who happened to work for one of those scandal sheets.'

'How terrible!' Melissa exclaimed. 'What did you do?'

He shrugged. 'What could I do? I fired her, of course, but the damage was already done. Any public figure is fair game for gossip. It's why I try to keep a low profile and guard what privacy I have so jealously.'

She nodded. 'Yes. I can understand that.' She smiled at him. 'I guess the price of fame can come pretty high.'

'Oh, yes,' he said with feeling.

He pushed himself away from the railing and stood gazing at her for a moment, a bemused expression on his lean, dark face, rubbing his chin thoughtfully. He's going to leave now, she thought in dismay, and searched her mind for something to say, anything to keep him there just a little while longer.

'Well,' he said at last. 'Do you feel up to one last dance?'

She stared at him, hardly able to believe her ears. 'Yes,' she finally managed. 'I'd like that.'

Smoothly and easily, he reached for her and she moved quite naturally into his arms. He held her loosely, one arm around her waist, clasping her hand with the other in the old-fashioned style, and away they went.

He turned out to be a marvellous dancer, nothing elaborate, but he led firmly and was quite easy to follow, every step sure and confident as he swept her around the deck. The music was a rather melancholy Mexican folk tune, slow and melodic, which seemed to fit the mood of the moment perfectly.

As they danced, Melissa felt as though she'd been wafted into a romantic fairyland. There could have been no more perfect ending to the voyage than to be dancing alone on a moonlit night with such a devastating man. It was a memory to treasure forever.

She was so absorbed in these happy thoughts that she didn't realise they had gradually been moving closer together until she felt his cheek on hers, slightly rough, and his warm breath in her ear.

Thrilled to the core, she allowed herself to relax in his arms even more closely up against him, and the feel of the long, hard body moving against hers as he guided her steps was awakening an unmistakable reaction in her, old sensations she'd believed were long buried.

The music stopped suddenly, but instead of releasing her, as she had expected, his arm stayed in place around her waist, his hand still holding hers. She looked up at him. He was turned so that his face was bathed in the moonlight now, and what she saw in the glittering silvery eyes almost took her breath away. Whatever romantic notions she'd secretly been harbouring were obviously on his mind too, and she waited, hardly daring to breathe, for what was coming.

He turned his head to look down at her, his eyes searching hers, holding them fast in a deep, penetrating gaze. Then slowly his dark head bent down towards her. She closed her eyes, and in the next moment felt his lips on hers, brushing gently against them at first, then gradually increasing the pressure.

Just then the music started up again. Without breaking the kiss or drawing away from her, he started to dance again. This time both arms were around her, one hand splayed on her bare back, the other clutching her tightly around the waist. She raised her own arms up and twined them around his neck, and as her fingers explored the back of his neck, the thick hair growing rather low, she felt the sharp intake of his breath, and the kiss deepened.

When he finally tore his lips from hers, it was to press light kisses along her cheek, her jawline, until his mouth came to rest just above her ear, buried in her hair. They danced that way for some time, locked together, their feet barely moving now, in more of a swaying motion than a dance.

Melissa felt as though she'd been transported to heaven, the exotic setting, the exciting man, the sheer bliss of the moment. She had a fleeting thought of Jack and his fumbling attempts at seduction, and it was like comparing a great artist with a rank amateur. Jack was only a boy. Miles Thatcher was a man.

It was then it struck her where all this was leading, and she had a moment's pause. Did she really want that? Was she ready for it? But it was too late for such questions. She was committed now, past the point of no return. Whatever he wanted from her she would give him.

She placed her hand on his face to trace the line of his jaw, then raised her arms around his neck again, running her fingers up through the crisp hair, pressing herself even more closely up against him in a gesture of total self-giving. His reading of her moods was so accurate that he couldn't possibly be in doubt what she was agreeing to, even offering him.

Then, suddenly, he pulled away from her, and his hands moved to grip her by the shoulders. She stood there gazing up at him with a heart full of love, waiting to see what he'd do.

Finally, he gave her a quirky smile. 'You know, Melissa,' he said in a dead serious tone, 'you're a very dangerous woman.'

Hardly able to believe her ears, her eyes flew open and she gave a nervous laugh. 'Who, me?'

He nodded. 'Yes, you.' His voice was low and soft, almost hypnotic. He put a hand on her cheek. 'There's something about your freshness and vulnerability that brings out a side of me I thought was dead forever. I think it's called tenderness,' he added lightly. 'And I'm not sure I can afford that.' He gave her a quirky smile and dropped his hand from her face. 'Now I think it's time to take you to your cabin.'

They walked slowly down the metal staircase to the deck below. Melissa's heart was pounding so hard that she thought he must be able to hear it. As she went before him down the stairs, his hands settled lightly on her shoulders, and the touch of his fingers on her bare skin made her head swim.

When they reached the door to her cabin, she fumbled in her handbag for the key, then with shaking fingers inserted it in the lock, opened it, and stepped inside. When he didn't follow her, she turned around and gave him a questioning look.

He was standing just outside the door, his head cocked to one side, his expression sober. 'Well, Melissa,' he said at last. 'I'll say goodnight now.'

She could only stare at him. What did he want from her, an engraved invitation? If she'd actually come right out and asked him inside, she couldn't have made her expectations clearer. And they certainly didn't include an abrupt goodnight at her door. Even with her meagre experience, she couldn't possibly have misjudged his intentions, his desire. Then what had gone wrong?

'I want you to know how much I've enjoyed our short acquaintance,' he was going on. 'You've been the one bright spot in an otherwise very boring trip.' He smiled thinly, gave her a brief nod, and backed away. 'And I wish you luck with your job-hunting,' he added as an afterthought.

The next thing she knew he was walking away from her, sauntering, actually, his hands in his pockets, whistling lightly under his breath, his air casual and confident. She stood there at the open door staring after him until he was lost from view, and she heard his footsteps resounding on the metal steps.

CHAPTER FOUR

'WELL, dear, how was the party last night?' asked
Frances the next morning at breakfast.

'Pretty dead,' Melissa replied. 'Most of the passengers were still recuperating from the effects of the
storm.'

'Yes, I was sorry to miss it myself. Was it a terrible
disappointment to you? I know how you were looking
forward to it.'

'Well, it wasn't everything I hoped it would be,
although it did liven up towards the end.' She laughed.
'Jack showed up and we had a great time dancing a
wicked tango.'

'Yes, I heard about that from Mrs Gregory. She said
you both seemed to be enjoying yourselves immensely.'

'It was fun,' Melissa replied. 'And quite a new sensation for me to be the centre of all that attention. Jack
was a little the worse for rum and Cokes, but did manage
a passable performance.'

'Did anyone else interesting show up?'

'Yes, the others began to straggle in around eleven
o'clock, but by then I'd had enough anyway and went
to my cabin early. Today we dock in San Diego, and I
haven't even begun to pack.'

'Well, I've certainly enjoyed getting to know you,
Melissa, and hope we can stay in touch. As you know,
I live in Monterey, which is only a few hours up the

coast from Santa Barbara. Perhaps we can get together some time.'

'Yes, of course. I'd like that.'

While they finished their breakfast, Melissa gazed around the room at the other passengers, all of whom had the same serious, subdued look about them that was typical at the end of a voyage as the time came to get back to reality.

There was no sign of Miles Thatcher, and after what had happened between them last night she was just as glad. Perhaps it had all been a dream, the moonlit dance on the deck, the kiss—then the let-down when he left her at the door of her cabin. Her cheeks still burned at the memory.

In any case, today she'd be going home, to an empty apartment and no employment. Her heart sank at the thought of the dreary round of job-hunting she would be faced with.

When they finished breakfast, she and Frances exchanged addresses and walked together down the stairs to the stateroom deck. At Melissa's door, they stopped for a moment.

'You know, Melissa,' said Frances, 'I think it's marvellous the way you've walked away with the prize male on this voyage. I'm sure you're the envy of all the other girls.'

Melissa gave her a swift glance. Could she be referring to Miles Thatcher? She didn't want to discuss that fiasco with anyone. No one had seen them together, however, so there was no reason for even the all-seeing, all-knowing Frances to have found out.

'What do you mean?' she asked at last.

'Why, your blond—what's the phrase? Hunk, I think it is. Yes. Your blond hunk. Jack.'

Melissa laughed. 'Oh, Jack. Yes, he's been fun, and I still can't imagine why he chose to hang around me instead of the much more glamorous women who are really trying.'

'Oh, I imagine he finds you restful,' she said. 'You do have that quality, you know. You don't fuss, or show off, and you know how to listen.'

Melissa felt a sharp pang. That was almost exactly what Miles had said about her. Was that such a wonderful compliment? Not desirable, not seductive, not beautiful—restful!

'Yes, well,' she said, opening her door, 'I don't imagine I'll be seeing him again, but I'll have to admit he did make the trip more enjoyable.'

They said goodbye then, with promises to get together soon, and Melissa went inside her cabin to face her packing. Since she was neat by nature, and without a lot of clothes to begin with, there wasn't that much to do. It was only nine-thirty, and since the ship wasn't scheduled to dock in San Diego until noon there was plenty of time. The passengers had been warned, however, that the stewards would come around early to collect their luggage, so she decided she might as well get started.

She had just finished clearing out her toilet articles from the bathroom and was putting them inside the small cosmetic case when there came a knock at the door.

'Oh, no!' she muttered, running over to answer it. She had no idea they'd come *this* early! She opened the door, all ready to tell the steward he'd just have to come back later, but it was Jack standing there, his hand raised to knock again.

'Jack!' she said. 'What are you doing here?'

He grinned. 'Well, I had to say goodbye, didn't I? And I'd like to have your address and telephone number. Hollywood isn't that far from Santa Barbara, and who knows? If I finally do give up my great acting career, they must sell shoes there, too, and I'm really not a bad salesman.'

She had to laugh. 'All right. Come on in for a minute and I'll write it out for you.'

He came inside and waited beside the open door while she scribbled her address on a sheet of ship stationery. 'There,' she said, handing it to him. She pointed at the letterhead. 'That's so you'll remember where you met me.'

He scowled. 'Come on, Melissa, I'm not that bad, am I?'

'No, of course not. I was only teasing you. It's been great fun getting to know you, Jack. And I really enjoyed our tango last night. I didn't think I had it in me.'

Suddenly he sobered. 'About last night,' he said carefully. 'Did I make an ass of myself again?'

'Not at all,' she reassured him. 'We just had a good time. I take it you stayed until the bitter end after the others showed up?'

'Afraid so. That's why I don't remember too much of what went on before.'

'Well, if you're really worried about it, you can set your mind at rest. We put on a great show, then I left early.'

'OK, if you say so.' He leaned down impulsively and gave her a quick peck on the cheek. 'It's been great, Melissa,' he said. 'And I will look you up one of these days. You can count on it.'

With a little wave, he stepped back into the corridor and Melissa shut the door after him. Smiling to herself, she continued with her packing until, half an hour later, there came another knock. This time her luggage was ready.

But it still wasn't the steward, but Miles Thatcher, the last person she expected—or wanted—to see. She simply stood there staring at him wordlessly, wondering what he could want with her now.

'May I come in?' he asked. 'I'd like to talk to you.'

'What about?' she asked hesitantly.

He smiled. 'Well, if you'll let me come in, just for a moment or two, I'll tell you.'

'All right,' she said. 'But I expect the steward will be along any moment for my bags, and I'm not quite finished packing.'

'It won't take long.'

He stepped inside, gave the small tidy cabin a cursory glance, then closed the door behind him and leaned back against it. He didn't say anything for a moment or two, then he came walking towards her until he'd covered the few steps between them.

Melissa's heart was pounding violently. He looked perfectly devastating this morning, dressed in a well-tailored business suit, crisp white shirt, dark tie. His face was tanned, and he was freshly shaven, his dark hair neatly brushed.

'I was wondering if you'd come to any decision about your job situation,' he said at last.

'No, I haven't,' she replied briskly. 'I told you. I'll start looking as soon as I get home.'

He just stood there, gazing pensively into space, chin in hand, his expression rather brooding, as though he was mulling something over in his mind. Melissa watched him warily, wondering what was up.

Finally the grey eyes flicked back at her. 'Well, then,' he said abruptly, 'how would you like to come to work for me?'

She goggled at him in utter astonishment. Taken completely off guard by the bizarre suggestion, she didn't know what to think, what to say. Her mind raced. Work for Miles Thatcher? On the one hand, it sounded like the most interesting job she could imagine, to work for a world-famous writer. On the other, there was something about the man that had a deeply unsettling effect on her. He seemed to possess a power over her she couldn't begin to fathom—or resist. And just what kind of duties did he have in mind?

'I don't know,' she finally said in a small voice. 'I mean, what would the job entail?'

'Nothing too onerous,' he replied. 'In fact, it would be much the same as what you've been doing. Taking dictation, handling correspondence, transcribing from a tape recorder, typing up my manuscripts.' He paused for a moment. 'Actually, your duties could encompass just about anything.'

'Like what?' she asked, immediately on guard.

He shrugged. 'Like running errands, dealing with reporters, fending off autograph hunters.' Then he grinned disarmingly. 'Perhaps even cooking from time to time. Can you cook?'

'Passably. Although,' she added swiftly, 'I'm not cordon bleu calibre.'

'I wouldn't expect you to be. I don't have exotic tastes in food.' He paused again, the smile faded and he gave her a sober look. 'Actually, there are a few aspects of the job that might give you trouble, and before you make up your mind I think I should warn you about them.'

'What are they?' she asked warily.

'Only two, actually. For one thing, my handwriting is virtually indecipherable.'

'And what's the other?' she said when he didn't go on.

He flashed her another wicked grin. 'My nasty disposition when I'm in the throes of the creative bug. It's sheer agony, believe me, and I tend to take it out on the object closest to hand.'

She had to smile. 'That surprises me. Your books read so smoothly that I figured you just tossed them off.'

He rolled his eyes heavenwards. 'Oh, if you only knew!' he said with feeling. 'Nothing could be further from the truth! You don't know the meaning of suffering until you try to write a book.'

'Why do you do it, then?' She spread her arms. 'I mean, you surely don't need the money, and you're famous enough already.'

'I can't answer that,' he said. 'It's like a fatal disease. Once bitten, you seem to be hooked for good.' His face hardened again. 'Well, what do you say? Think you'd be interested?'

She turned away from him, biting her lip and staring out through the grimy porthole for a few seconds. Did she want to or didn't she? Somehow she sensed danger. But she'd played it safe all her life and where had it got her? She really had nothing to lose.

Finally she turned around to face him. 'All right,' she said. 'I'm game to try if you are. I just hope you won't be disappointed.'

'Why should I be disappointed?' Suddenly his eyes narrowed suspiciously. 'You do have secretarial skills, don't you?'

'Oh, yes. I think I can handle that aspect of the job. Even,' she added, grinning, 'the cooking.'

'Well, then?'

She raised her chin and gave him a level look. 'It's just that I have the sneaking feeling you'd be a very demanding boss, and I should warn *you* that there are limits to what I'll put up with in the way of temperament.'

He threw back his head and laughed. 'That's what I like about you, Melissa. You say what you think. Besides, as I told you before, I find you a very restful person.'

Thanks a lot! she thought bitterly. There was that hateful word again. It was on the tip of her tongue to ask him if it was her 'restful' qualities that had prompted him to dance with her last night, to kiss her, to *almost* come inside her cabin with her. But if she really was going to take the job, that would definitely be starting out on the wrong foot.

'Now,' he was saying briskly. 'As to the details.' He named a salary that was at least double what she'd been paid at her last job, and that fact alone was enough to convince her she'd made the right decision. 'Will that be adequate? If you work out as well as I hope, of course, and can take more responsibility off my shoulders, there would be periodic raises.'

'Yes,' she said in a choked voice. 'That will be adequate.'

'There's one more thing,' he said slowly. 'I work odd hours, and need a secretary who's willing to be on call pretty much twenty-four hours a day.'

For the money he was willing to pay her that didn't sound at all unreasonable. 'All right,' she said, nodding. 'I've no problem with that.'

'In that case,' he went on in a measured tone, 'how would you feel about living in my house?'

For a moment she wasn't sure she'd heard him right. 'What did you say?' was all she could manage.

'I said I think it would be more convenient if you lived in my house. I have far more room than I need, and it would save a lot of going back and forth, sometimes in the middle of the night.'

She searched his face for some sign of what was going on behind that bland mask. Just what 'duties' did he have in mind? She wasn't about to get caught in *that* trap again. The man was like quicksilver, hot on the trail one minute, cold as ice the next. If she really was going to work for him, she'd need all her wits about her just to keep her balance.

In fact, she had to wonder if she hadn't already made a terrible mistake by agreeing to take the job in the first place. It still wasn't too late to back out.

'I don't know if that would be such a good idea,' she finally replied.

He frowned and gave her the unsettling penetrating look that meant he was reading her mind again, then laughed drily. 'Oh, you don't have to worry about *that*. My housekeeper lives in, and she makes a very efficient chaperon.'

Melissa reddened. His uncanny ability to know her thoughts was unnerving, and once again she considered backing out. But to do what? And the salary he was offering, not to mention a place to live, was too tempting to pass up.

But actually to live with him in his house? Melissa bit her lip and stared down at her feet, thinking furiously. Housekeeper or not, she had serious doubts about that, especially after the short romantic interlude last night. Granted it hadn't really led anywhere serious, and nothing irrevocable had happened—still, it almost had, and if she was going to work for him that kind of thing would have to be strictly out of bounds.

The sound of his footsteps coming towards her snapped her out of her inner debate, and she raised her eyes to see that he was standing before her, his head cocked to one side, his face guarded, but with a smile on his lips.

'If you're worried about what happened last night,' he said in a low voice, 'you can set your mind at rest. Let's just say we both got a little carried away with the moonlight, and leave it at that. What do you say?'

Her eyes searched his. He *seemed* sincere enough. And the smile was kindly, not mocking. He needed a secretary. She needed a job. Wasn't that pretty simple?

'All right,' she said at last. 'I've no objection to giving it a try.' She gave him a cool glance. 'I guess if you can keep your head, so can I.'

His eyes widened momentarily, then his features relaxed and he grinned at her. 'That's another thing I like about you. You never fail to surprise me.' He turned and started walking towards the door, then stopped and glanced back at her. 'I've arranged for a car to meet me at the harbour in San Diego,' he said in a clipped voice. 'You'll ride up with me to Santa Barbara.'

With that he was gone, the door closed quietly behind him. Melissa stood in the middle of the tiny cabin for several long moments, wondering if she'd made a wise decision that could mean a once-in-a-lifetime experience, or just taken the most disastrous step of her life.

The ship docked at noon, right on schedule. Melissa was up on deck as they pulled into the busy harbour, searching for Miles, who was nowhere to be seen in the bustling crowds that lined the railings waving at the people standing below who had come to meet them.

She'd told the steward when he came for her luggage to put it with Mr Thatcher's, but now she wondered if that had been such a good idea. If she couldn't find him, there was no telling where her suitcase would end up.

Then, finally, she spotted him. He was walking briskly towards her, dark glasses in place, his face set, even rather grim. He came up to stand beside her and flicked her a quick sideways glance.

'There's a crowd of reporters down there at the foot of the gangway,' he said in a low, curt voice. 'Do you see them?'

She glanced over the railing and saw that indeed there was a group of men dressed in rumpled suits, gazing intently up at the approaching ship, scanning the crowd of passengers on the deck.

'Yes,' she said. 'I see them.'

'I'll have to deal with them, and I'd like you close by, but in case we get separated that's my driver standing about ten feet behind them, the small Latino in the dark suit and white shirt. His name's Pedro.'

She nodded. 'All right.'

'Come on, then,' he said, taking her by the arm. 'Let's go.'

She fell into step beside him and, when they reached the top of the gangway, moved behind him. Slowly, they inched their way down with the other passengers.

Looking past Miles, she could see the three newsmen down below gazing up eagerly, their eyes fastened on Miles.

'Mr Thatcher, Mr Thatcher!' someone called. And they began shouting at him, one staccato question after another. 'Was this a holiday or a business trip? Why were you travelling incognito? Is there a romance in the offing? What's the title of your next book? Is the last one going to be made into a film? Who's the star to be? How about that television series we've been hearing rumours about?'

Melissa stood off to one side, watching him with something like awe as he deftly parried the barrage of questions. He was smiling, gracious, but quite firm in his replies and obviously an old hand at this kind of thing.

After about twenty minutes, however, she could tell that he'd had enough. His face got that familiar set, closed-in look, and his strong chin was lifted determinedly. Out of the corner of her eyes, she could see Pedro coming up beside him, silent and watchful.

'All right,' Miles said in a brusque, commanding tone. 'That'll be all, gentlemen. I have to leave now for an urgent appointment.' He flicked a glance at Melissa, gripped her firmly by the arm, and positioned her in front of him. 'This is my secretary,' he said to them over her head. 'If you have more questions, she'll fill in the details.'

Startled, she swivelled her head around and gave him a horrified look. 'Me!' she whispered fiercely, so that only he could hear. 'But I don't know how to do that! What shall I say?'

'That's up to you,' he muttered. 'I don't care. Come on, you'll do fine.' He gave her a humourless smile. 'Consider it your first assignment.'

She narrowed her eyes at him. 'Well, then you'd better make sure I'm on the payroll as of right now,' she said through her teeth, 'because I have a feeling I'm going to have to earn it the hard way.'

He chuckled. 'That's the spirit. I'll meet you at the car.'

He deftly side-stepped the group of men, gave them a little salute and, with Pedro running interference, strode briskly away. Melissa, still stunned, gazed after him for a moment, then turned slowly around to face the reporters, who were clearly losing interest fast now that Miles had outmanoeuvred them. If she didn't come up with something, they'd simply chase after him.

Having no idea what in the world to say, she cleared her throat loudly and blurted out the first thing that came into her head. 'Mr Thatcher has asked me to make a statement for him.'

Their heads came round immediately and three pairs of eyes gazed at her with deep suspicion.

'I'm Mr Thatcher's secretary,' she declared stoutly. 'And he has asked me to tell you——' She broke off, hesitating. Tell them what? They were already looking bored. 'To tell you,' she went on in a loud voice, 'that the purpose of his trip to Mexico was to do research for his new book.'

That got their attention. They crowded in closer to her, pencils and notebooks poised, and began to hurl questions at her. The title, the subject, the plot, the meaning. Overwhelmed by it all, she simply threw caution to the winds and made up answers as she went along, having no idea whether they were fact or fiction. He could only kill her once, after all. Or it might well turn out to be the first time in history that a person was fired from a job before even starting it.

Finally satisfied, the reporters began to drift away. It seemed that a famous actress was about to appear at a nearby dock, and that meant they'd leave Miles alone, at least this time.

When they were gone, she looked around, wondering what she was supposed to do next. Beyond the tall metal fence enclosing the docking area was a car park, and she headed towards it as the most likely place to find him. Sure enough, on the other side of the gate sat a long, sleek car, its motor running, apparently waiting for her.

As she stood there, still undecided, the back door on her side opened. She hurried towards it and jumped inside. Immediately, the car moved forward.

The drive up the coast was a silent one. Melissa and Miles sat in the back on the spacious leather-upholstered seat, while Pedro sat alone in the front.

Melissa had never been inside such a luxurious car. She couldn't even guess how much it cost, but had a vague idea it was probably many times what she had ever earned in a year. It smelled heavenly, and every inch was spotless, every chrome fixture gleaming, the tinted windows clear as crystal.

Before they'd even cleared the harbour, Miles had already opened his briefcase and become deeply immersed in a thick sheaf of papers, all of them closely covered with slashing black handwriting. From time to time as they rode along she tried to sneak a look at them out of the corner of her eye to see just how hard it was going to be to read, but without much luck.

When she realised that neither of the men had any intention of speaking to her, she decided she might as well relax and enjoy the ride. The silence suited her anyway. It was soothing not to have to make small talk, and after Pedro had manoeuvred the car through the intricate interchanges in the Los Angeles area she leaned back and gazed out of the window at the small towns as they whizzed by.

It wasn't until they arrived on the outskirts of Santa Barbara that Miles finally looked up from his papers. He had a rather dazed look on his face, like a man who had suddenly been transported from his own private universe into the real world. He blinked a few times, frowning, then glanced out of the window, as though to re-orientate himself.

Finally, he shuffled the pages on his lap into a neat pile, tamping down the edges until they were even, and replaced them in the briefcase at his feet. Then he turned to her.

'You'll have to give Pedro directions to your place. He can drop you off, then come back to pick you up later. How long do you think it will take you to pack?'

She stared at him. 'You mean tonight?'

He nodded. 'Do you have a problem with that?'

'Well, yes. I can't possibly get everything taken care of today.'

'I don't see why not.' His tone was reasonable, but firm.

She glanced at her watch. 'But it's already past three o'clock.'

'How long does it take to pack a few clothes? You've probably got all you need in your suitcases right now, as a matter of fact.

'But it's not just the packing,' she protested, really rather alarmed now at the way he was pressuring her. She began to tick off on her fingers. 'I have to speak to the manager about cancelling my lease, get the telephone turned off, empty the refrigerator...' She broke off and made a helpless gesture. 'There are all kinds of little things one has to do to move. I can't just walk out.'

'Oh, well,' he said, leaning back and closing his eyes. 'You can take care of all that later. I want to start working on the new book tomorrow, and will need you right away.'

She knew there was no point in arguing with him about it. And he was right. It wasn't really necessary to take care of every detail today. Still, she felt a little uneasy about the way he was sweeping her off her feet and into a commitment she still wasn't quite sure she was ready to make. It was one thing to take a cautious step into the unknown, the alien world this man inhabited, but quite another to be pushed into it before she had a chance to think it over.

Then she realised that her old cautious self was getting the upper hand again. She'd decided she was going to have an adventure, take the risk, plunge in with both feet. She actually had nothing to lose, and she wasn't exactly cutting off her head.

She leaned forward to give Pedro directions to her apartment, and after a few minutes he pulled up in front of the building. Before getting out she glanced over at Miles, but his eyes were still closed and he seemed to be sleeping quite peacefully. Then she heard Pedro asking her what time she wanted him to come back for her. What she needed, she thought wryly, was a week, but she'd take whatever she could get.

'Would nine o'clock be all right?' she asked hesitantly. 'Or is that too late for you?'

He twisted his head around and smiled. 'You tell me when you want me to come, and I'll be here.'

'All right, then,' she said opening her door and stepping out on to the pavement. 'Nine o'clock.'

She was just about to close the door when Miles leaned across the seat and peered up at her. 'By the way,' he said, 'what did you tell those reporters?'

'Oh, I just made up some things. That's what you told me to do,' she added defensively when she saw the dubious look on his face.

He only nodded, then reached out to pull the door closed, and the next thing she knew she was standing on the pavement all alone watching the sleek car race off down the street. She had no choice now. Just about everything she owned was packed in suitcases which were now stowed in the trunk of that car.

When the car finally disappeared from view around the corner, she sighed deeply and started walking up the path.

By nine o'clock, she'd done as much as she could in just a few short hours. Actually she'd already cleaned quite thoroughly before leaving on her trip, so there wasn't that much to do. She spoke to her landlord, who informed her that he didn't think he'd have any trouble subletting her apartment, so at least she didn't have to worry about the four months the lease still had to run.

By the time Pedro pulled up outside, on the dot of nine, she was as ready as she'd ever be. She had put everything she wanted to take in plastic carrier bags and was able to manage them on her own. She gave her tiny living-room one last glance, switched off the lights and went out into the hallway, locking the door behind her.

Pedro was already standing on the pavement waiting for her. Silently he took the bags from her, and after putting them in the car he opened the back door for her.

'Couldn't I sit in the front with you?' she asked. 'I'd feel strange sitting back there all by myself.'

He nodded. 'Sure,' he said. 'Whatever you want.'

On the way, she tried to make conversation with him, to draw him out about Miles, but although he was unfailingly polite and pleasant she learned exactly nothing, so skilful was he in avoiding giving out information about him.

Although this disappointed her, she was also impressed by how well-trained the boy was. Clearly he'd learned early that if he wanted to keep his job the first requisite was never, in any circumstances, to discuss his employer, not even with his secretary.

Soon they were travelling up a winding street that led into the foothills to the east of town, until they came to a tall, wrought-iron gate. Pedro stopped, pushed a button on the dashboard, and the gates swung open. He drove through on to a narrow paved road that circled around cultivated garden areas.

There were lights up ahead, and as they approached them she could make out the contours of a house, long and low. The closer they came, the larger the house looked, and by the time Pedro stopped outside it she'd realised it was far more extensive than it had appeared at first sight.

It was built of pale stucco, in the Spanish style, with a red tiled roof. Under the eaves of the wide veranda that stretched completely across the front of the house were heavy dark oak beams. Red clay pots filled with flowers hung from them, and at the sides of the wide, polished double front doors were two large adobe urns, also full of bright blooms. The fixtures on the doors, the lamps, the low bench beside them were made of wrought iron, painted black.

Pedro had come around to her side of the car to open the door for her, leaving the motor running, and when she stepped outside she was struck immediately by the eerie silence. Except for the low hum of the car engine as Pedro drove off and the distant chirping of crickets, there wasn't a sound.

Then the front door opened, and a short, stout, dark-haired woman of indeterminate age came outside, smiling broadly and beckoning to Melissa.

'Welcome, Miss Ryder,' she said.

'Oh, Melissa, please.'

The woman nodded. 'OK, and I'm Maria, Mr Thatcher's housekeeper. Come inside and I'll take you to your room. Have you eaten?' She spoke with just a trace of a Spanish accent, and Melissa wondered if she and Pedro were related.

'Yes, thank you,' Melissa replied, following her inside to a spacious entrance hall paved in red quarry tile.

'Follow me, then,' Maria said.

Melissa followed her down a wide corridor that seemed to go on forever, with so many twists and turns that she knew she'd never be able to find her way back. Finally they came to an open door, and Maria stopped, pointing inside.

'This will be your room,' she said. 'The bed is all made up, and the bathroom is through that door. I don't think I've forgotten anything, but if I have please let me know.'

Just then Pedro came down the hall carrying the plastic bags she'd taken from her apartment. They looked terribly tacky against the quiet elegance of the house, and she reached for them as soon as he came to the door, anxious to get them out of sight.

'Thank you, Pedro,' she said. 'And you, too, Maria.'

What she wanted most of all now was to be alone, to digest this strange new world she'd entered so abruptly. Her head was still whirling with the suddenness of it all.

Pedro was already hurrying off down the hall, and Maria stepped back from the door, clearly intending to go.

'I'll leave you to get settled now,' she said. 'Sleep as long as you want tomorrow. You must be tired after your long trip today.'

'Thank you. I will.'

Melissa closed the door and stood there for a moment gazing around at her new home. It was an enormous room, so large that her whole apartment would have fitted inside it. The floors were polished oak, with rugs scattered about, and it was very simply furnished with a double bed covered in a brightly coloured Mexican spread, a dark oak bureau, a dressing-table with a framed mirror, a few comfortable chairs and a table by the window. The walls were white plaster, the curtains made out of a rough white material.

Her two large suitcases, which she had packed just that morning on the ship, were set on a low carved wooden chest next to the bed. Suddenly a wave of exhaustion passed over her. There was no way she could face unpacking tonight.

She went over and opened one of the bags to get her nightclothes, then undressed hurriedly, letting her clothes fall where they lay, something ordinarily unthinkable to her neat nature. She pulled back the covers of the bed, switched off the bedside lamp and climbed in.

As she lay there in the dark, in the few seconds before she fell into a sound and dreamless sleep, her one thought was how lucky she was to have fallen into this job, in this beautiful house, with this man, and how determined she was to do her best to please him so that she could keep it all.

CHAPTER FIVE

IT WAS the next morning at breakfast that the storm burst.

Melissa rose early, anxious to get a proper start on her first day at work and to make a good impression on her volatile employer. After her bath, she got dressed in one of the neat but rather threadbare cotton shirt-dresses.

By the time she'd unpacked her suitcases and put her clothes and toilet articles away, it was still only eight o'clock. She went out into the hall and began to creep along the seemingly endless maze of corridors, hoping to come across some sign of life in the deathly quiet house.

Finally she heard low voices, the sound of a radio playing a Latin American tune, the rattle of crockery. Heading in that direction, and guided by the heavenly aroma of fresh coffee and frying bacon, she finally found the kitchen.

Maria was at the stove cooking, and Pedro was sitting at a round table by the window, which overlooked the side-garden, brilliant in the early morning sunshine with colourful bougainvillaea and hibiscus blooms surrounding an immaculate lawn with a large pond set in the middle of it. There was no sign of Miles.

'Excuse me,' she called timidly from the doorway.

Pedro looked up from his breakfast, and Maria turned around to give her a broad smile. 'Come in, come in,' she said cheerily. 'You'll be wanting your breakfast.'

'Well, yes, I am rather hungry.' Melissa stepped inside and nodded at Pedro, who had already leapt to his feet. 'Oh,' she said, crossing over to the table, 'don't let me disturb you.'

'I've finished,' the boy said. He turned to Maria. 'You'll let me know when you want me to take you shopping, Mamá?'

'This afternoon, I think,' Maria replied. 'I'll call you.'

Pedro nodded, then turned to Melissa, gave her a shy smile, and went outside through the kitchen door. When he was gone, Melissa went over to the stove, where Maria was just turning over the sizzling rashers.

'You want one egg or two?' she asked.

'Well, two, I guess,' Melissa replied. 'But I can fix my own breakfast. You don't need to wait on me.' She laughed. 'I'm not used to it, believe me.'

'No, no,' Maria said firmly. 'I don't like anyone else cooking in my kitchen. You sit down. It'll only be a minute.'

Melissa headed meekly back to the table, but paused halfway there and turned around. 'Maybe I should wait for Miles,' she said.

'Oh, no,' Maria replied as she expertly broke eggs into the pan. 'Mr Thatcher already had breakfast in his study. He takes all his meals in there when he's working.' She nodded towards the coffee-maker on the counter beside her. 'You can pour yourself a cup now if you want.'

'Thanks, I could use some.'

She had just poured it out and was carrying it back to the table when Miles appeared in the doorway. She set the cup down and smiled at him, about to wish him a good morning, but the expression on his face stopped her cold. It was thunderous, the heavy dark eyebrows set in a forbidding scowl, the thin mouth set, the grey eyes snapping.

He was holding a newspaper in one hand, his arm upraised, waving it in the air. He came walking slowly towards her, his tread measured, until he stood before her, looming over her. Looking up into his face, she could see that he was literally speechless with fury, which for some reason seemed to be directed squarely at her.

Melissa set her cup down carefully on the table. 'Is something wrong?' she finally managed to ask in a small voice.

'Wrong?' he shouted. 'Wrong!'

He raised the paper again, gave it an even more violent shake, and for a moment Melissa was positive he meant to give her a good hard smack with it. Then, just as suddenly, his face crumpled and he sank down into a chair, put his elbows on the table and covered his head in his hands, groaning piteously.

Melissa could only stand there, wringing her hands, in an agony of confusion and anxiety. She glanced over at Maria, only to see that her back was turned, her head bowed, studiously ignoring the whole scene.

Finally Miles raised his head and gave her a look of such deep scorn that it chilled her to the bone. He slapped the newspaper down on the table and pointed a dramatic finger at it.

'Do you have any idea what you've done?' he snarled. 'Here,' he barked, picking it up again and shoving it at her. 'Read that.'

Still totally bewildered, Melissa gingerly reached out and took it from him. It was the local newspaper, turned to an inside page. She scanned the columns frantically, the type swimming before her eyes, trying to focus on what it was he found so offensive. When she finally spotted a photograph of Miles, it slowly began to sink in just what all the fuss was about.

As she concentrated hard on the wavering lines of type below the picture, her heart sank lower and her cheeks burned brighter with every word she read. In the article was a rather lengthy description of Miles's new book, a book she had manufactured herself out of whole cloth. Setting, characters, background, purpose, all set out in meticulous detail, just as she had announced it to the reporters yesterday at the San Diego harbour.

Finally, red-faced, her heart thudding heavily, she glanced at Miles. He was leaning back in the chair, his arms folded across his chest, his burning eyes fixed on her. She hadn't a clue what she could possibly say to him to make it all right, didn't even know where to begin. She'd been caught red-handed in a pack of blatant lies about a man who valued his privacy above everything else, and there was nothing she could do about it now but take her medicine.

There was utter silence in the room. Even Maria, still at the stove, didn't move a muscle. Melissa just stood there helplessly, speechless, waiting for him to lash out at her again.

'Well?' he barked. 'Would you care to offer me some explanation before I fire you?'

Melissa groaned inwardly. Fired on her first day of work! And she'd already given up her apartment, brought everything she owned here. What was she going to do now? It wasn't fair!

Then, deep within her, a little spark of anger slowly began to ignite. After all, he was the one who'd left her at the mercy of those reporters while he made his getaway. Now he was blaming her for what she'd said. The tiny spark blazed a little higher, stiffening her spine and giving her courage.

'Yes,' she said in a dead even voice. 'I would.'

Miles's eyes flickered momentarily, obviously taken aback by the calm statement. He waved a hand towards the chair opposite him. 'Very well,' he said. 'Let's hear it.'

Slowly, taking her time, tucking her dress underneath her, she sat down, folded her hands primly before her on top of the table, and gave him a direct, level gaze. Still shaking inside and hoping it wouldn't show in her voice, she began to speak.

'I'm sorry if I made a mistake,' she began hesitantly. Then, hearing that her voice was steady after all, she went on more firmly, 'But if you'll remember, you yourself told me you didn't care what I said, just so long as I kept those reporters distracted while you and Pedro went to the car. You didn't tell me what to say, and I realised right away that I wasn't going to hold their attention for two seconds unless I gave them something interesting. So,' she added with a shrug, 'I just said the first thing that came into my head.'

'I see,' he said through his teeth. He tilted his chair back, crossed his arms over his chest and gave her a withering look. 'Maybe you'd like to write the book as well.'

For a moment, as their eyes locked together in mortal combat, and in spite of her own rising anger, Melissa once again felt cowed by his assurance. After all, this was a world-famous man, sought after by the media. In any battle of wills, surely he'd be right. She didn't quite accept that, however. She had her own dignity, her own integrity. It didn't matter how exalted his status in the world, he had no right to treat her like a disobedient, rather stupid child.

Slowly she rose to her feet, squared her shoulders and raised her chin. 'Very well,' she said icily. 'Since I'm fired, I guess I'd better go pack my things.'

Without another glance, she turned and marched sedately past him to the door. It wasn't until she was out in the corridor that she allowed her shoulders to sag, her face to crumple and the hot tears stinging behind her eyes to fall unchecked.

Blindly she stumbled down the maze of corridors in what she hoped was the right direction, getting lost in the process twice, until she finally reached her own bedroom. Or what used to be her own bedroom.

She went inside, slammed the door behind her, locked it securely, then retrieved her two empty suitcases. She set them on top of the bed and began throwing clothes inside any which way, sweeping dresses off the rack in the wardrobe, scooping underwear out of drawers.

She was sobbing openly by now, the hurt, angry tears streaming unchecked down her burning cheeks. He had no right to treat her that way! In front of Maria, too!

When she'd finished packing she went into the bathroom to wash her face, and stared at her reflection in the mirror over the washbasin, red-faced, teary-eyed, sniffling loudly. What a sorry end to her glamorous new job this turned out to be!

She began to splash cold water on her face, still muttering and grumbling to herself. She should have known better than to tie herself to a man like Miles Thatcher. He was nothing but an arrogant, egotistical, self-centred bully, a male chauvinist pig of the first rank.

After she'd dried off and combed her hair, she felt much better. The first thing she had to do was call a taxi so that she could get out of here—maybe leave some money by the telephone to pay for the call as a parting gesture—then go and see if she could get her old apartment back.

Just then there came a light rapping on her door. Miles, she thought grimly, determined to get the last word in. Well, let him! She wasn't afraid of him. There wasn't anything more he could do to her, and if he got really ugly she still had a few choice comments of her own to make.

She marched over to the door and flung it open, all ready to do battle again, but it was only Maria. She was carrying a tray, with a steaming pot of coffee, a glass of orange juice and a covered dish. She was also grinning from ear to ear.

'Here,' she said. 'I brought your breakfast.'

'Oh, thank you, Maria, but I'm afraid I've lost my appetite. I don't think I could eat a thing now.'

'Sure you can.' Maria moved past her, set the tray down on the dressing table, then glanced at the overflowing suitcases on the bed. 'You're going somewhere?' she asked.

'Of course I am. I certainly can't stay in this house another minute.'

Maria laughed. 'Oh, don't mind him. He blows up like that, then forgets it right away.' She shrugged. 'He's an artist.'

'Maria, he *fired* me!'

Maria waved a hand in the air. 'He's fired me and Pedro maybe twenty, thirty times in the five years we've been with him. At first we were like you, mad, scared, packing our bags, ready to go.' She shrugged. 'We don't pay any attention to him any more.'

Melissa shook her head. 'I can't do that. Besides, even though there's no excuse for the way he behaved, I have to admit he was probably right. I really shouldn't have said what I did to those reporters. I just can't handle the job, that's all.'

Just then Miles himself appeared in the doorway. He stood there, stone-faced, glancing from one woman to the other for several seconds. Then he cleared his throat loudly.

'If you don't mind, Maria,' he began in a lofty tone, 'I'd like to speak to Melissa alone for a minute.'

'Sure, boss,' Maria replied cheerfully. She winked at Melissa, then slid past Miles out into the corridor, humming loudly as she went.

'May I come in?' Miles asked.

'It's your house,' Melissa replied shortly.

'But this room is still your private territory.'

She looked at him. All his fury seemed to have been spent, and he looked almost apologetic. Almost, but not quite. There was still the same arrogant lift to his head, the same self-assured set of his shoulders. But at least it didn't look as though he'd come here to continue the battle.

'All right,' she said grudgingly at last. 'Come in, then.'

As he stepped inside he gave the suitcases one swift glance. He scowled darkly at them, then darted his eyes at Melissa, who stood quite still, not uttering a word. She'd said all she was going to. Finally, he took another step towards her.

'As soon as you finish unpacking, I'd like to have you come to my study so I can fill you in on your secretarial duties.'

Melissa stared at him. 'I thought you said I was fired,' she said stiffly.

'I know what I said.' There was a trace of irritation in his voice, but in the next instant he smiled. 'I say a lot of things I don't mean. That's something you'll just have to get used to.'

She sighed and looked away. 'I don't know, Miles,' she said slowly. 'Maybe it would be best for me to leave.'

'But I don't want you to go,' he said in a low voice.

She gave him a swift look. 'You don't?' He shook his head. 'I don't understand,' she went on. 'I'm obviously not up to the job. You said so yourself, and I'm inclined to agree with you.'

'All right,' he said, exasperated. 'I might have been wrong. I shouldn't have blown up at you that way. And

HARLEQUIN MILLS & BOON
LIMITED

Dear Reader,

Get out a coin–and go to work on the
WIN-A-FORTUNE tickets enclosed.
You could end up £600,000 richer!

By returning these tickets you'll also be
in the running for hundreds of other cash
prizes we'll be giving away. It costs
nothing to play –there's no fee, and no
purchase is necessary!

We're holding this prize draw to introduce
you to the benefits of the Reader Service.
Scratch off the gold boxes on the enclosed
Lucky 7 Slot Machine Game and we'll
send you free books and a cuddly teddy!

How many FREE BOOKS will you get?
Play the Slot Machine Game and see!
These books are absolutely free, with no
obligation to buy anything!

The Reader Service is **not** like some book
clubs. We charge you nothing for your
first shipment. And you don't have to make
any minimum number of purchases–not
even one!

over, please

FOLD ALONG DOTTED LINE AND DETACH CAREFULLY

For example, you could accept your FREE BOOKS and cancel immediately, by writing "please cancel" on the shipping label and returning it to us. You'll owe nothing and be under no further obligation!

But the fact is, thousands of readers enjoy receiving books by mail from the Reader Service. They look forward to getting the best new romance novels at least a month before they arrive in the shops. And <u>postage and packing is free!</u>

I'm hoping that after receiving your free books you'll want to remain a subscriber. But the choice is yours–to continue or cancel, any time at all!

Susan Welland

Susan Welland, for Reader Service

P.S. If you're accepting free books, play the 'Ace of Hearts' game for a free MYSTERY GIFT!

your point was well taken. I did throw you to the wolves yesterday. I can hardly blame you for what you told them, and there's actually no real harm done.' Then he smiled. 'In fact, with your vivid imagination, you might want to write your own book one of these days.'

'But you said...'

He held up a hand. 'Never mind what I said. Now, why don't you eat your breakfast, finish your un-packing, and take the rest of the morning off? You can start work this afternoon.'

As though the matter was all settled, he turned and strode towards the door. Melissa debated. She *should* leave. It would serve him right. But in spite of his ap-palling behaviour she really wanted to stay. Besides, at this point, with her apartment probably already sublet and no other job in sight, what did she have to lose?

'Then I take it I'm not fired?' she called after him.

Slowly he turned around. 'No,' he said. 'You're not.' Then he gave her a grim, tight-lipped smile. 'I might wring your neck if you ever pull a stunt like that again, but I meant it when I said I didn't want you to go.'

Later that day, after eating lunch in the kitchen with Maria and Pedro, and armed with directions from Maria, she presented herself at Miles's study, as he'd requested. The door was open, but there was no sign of Miles. She hesitated for a moment, then stepped inside and looked around.

It was obviously a room to work in. Except for the fireplace and a large window that overlooked a paved terrace and the good-sized swimming-pool, every inch of wall-space was covered with bookcases. In several of the empty spaces between the volumes were set framed photographs, and as Melissa wandered around examining them more carefully she could see that most of them were of famous people—a senator, a five-star general, even one president—all of them with short messages of gratitude. For what? His books, most likely.

In the middle of the room, facing the fireplace, was a large oak desk, piled high with stacks of paper, file folders, more books. In one corner was an enormous globe, in another a comfortable-looking leather chair with a lamp beside it.

There was a long, narrow library table in front of the window. On top of it was a typewriter, a neat stack of stenographer's notebooks, a ceramic mug holding several newly sharpened pencils and ball point pens, and, off to one side, a tape recorder.

She heard footsteps approaching in the hall and turned around to see Miles standing in the doorway, a half-smile on his face.

'Well?' he said. 'What do you think?'

'I think it's very impressive,' she said stiffly, still smarting a little from the morning's battle.

He came over and gestured towards the library table. 'This will be yours,' he said. 'I think you'll find everything you need.'

'Yes, I think so.'

'Anything else you want, just ask Maria, and she'll pick it up for you next time she goes shopping.'

'All right. I will.'

She turned away from that steady grey gaze, as a sudden shadow of doubt clouded her mind, a wave of shyness. Somehow all this efficiency, the businesslike ambience of the room, the photographs, intimidated her. Would she really be able to handle it?

He leaned his narrow hips back against the edge of the table and crossed his arms over his chest. 'Now, there's nothing to be nervous about, Melissa,' he said, once again reading her mind. 'We got off to a bad start this morning, but I think you'll find I'm not usually so difficult. I won't put you to work today, but I did want to get a few things clearly spelled out right from the beginning so there won't be any misunderstanding about my requirements.'

'Yes,' she said, nodding. 'I think that's a good idea.'

'The first, and most important thing,' he went on, 'is that when I need you here I want you available. Although I use a tape recorder, I'm not entirely comfortable with a machine, and there are times I like to dictate in person. That could mean any time of the day or night.'

'I understand,' she said, hoping she really did.

Then he gave her a warm, encouraging smile. 'Although I think I can promise you that I won't be getting you out of bed at two o'clock in the morning very often.'

The smile transformed him, made him seem more like the Miles she'd known on the ship, comfortable to be with. She'd had glimpses then of a softer, more understanding side to his nature. His quiet confidence calmed her nerves, and she was beginning to get excited again at the challenge of pleasing this enigmatic man.

'Now, are there any questions?' he asked.

She thought a moment. 'I can't think of any at the moment.'

'I'm sure you will in time,' he commented drily. He pushed himself away from the table and glanced out of the window. 'Now, why don't you take the rest of the day to find your way around, get settled? I may need you to take some dictation after dinner this evening, and I'll want all your attention.'

After such an inauspicious beginning, the days that followed were much easier by comparison. In fact as time passed Melissa came to believe that it was probably just as well she'd had her trial by fire at the very start of her employment.

It had been terrible—near fatal to the job, in fact—but it had taught her an important lesson, that her greatest challenge was handling Miles and his volatile temperament, at least when he was in the throes of creation. In fact the actual work she did, demanding as it was, seemed like child's play in comparison. She learned early on, however, not to take it personally. Although he blew easily, sometimes over trifles, it was always just as quickly forgotten.

She could see too why he wanted her to live in his house. At any time of the day or night, he would suddenly decide he needed her, and she'd been there for only a week when she had her first experience of it. It was late one night, and after a particularly tiring day she was just emerging from a long soak in the bath-tub when she heard him out in the corridor just outside her bedroom calling her name.

'Melissa!' he roared. 'I need you.'

She grabbed a towel off the rack and began drying off hastily. 'Just a minute, Miles,' she called. 'I just got out of the tub.'

'Well, get a move on. I'll be in the study.'

She threw on some clothes, ran a comb through her hair, put on a quick dab of lipstick and ran down the maze of corridors to his study. He was inside, pacing back and forth. Quietly she settled herself at her table by the window, pencil poised over her notebook.

He was in full spate tonight, talking so fast that her hand was virtually paralysed when he finally paused for breath. She looked up from her notebook, hoping she'd got everything down, but afraid to ask him to repeat anything.

He was slumped in the chair behind his desk, his head back, his eyes closed. Melissa waited. Finally he heaved a deep sigh, straightened up and gave her a suspicious look.

'Did you get all that?' he demanded.

'I—I think so.'

'You think so!' he thundered, half rising out of his chair. Then with a heroic effort he sat back down and folded his hands in front of him. 'Perhaps it would help,' he said in a tight voice, 'if you read a little of it back to me.'

As she slowly flipped back a few pages to a part where she was fairly confident she'd taken it down accurately, her hands were shaking and her heart pounding. Then she began to read, and to her amazement it came out sounding pretty much the way he'd dictated it.

'All right,' he broke in after a few pages. 'That's all right, then. Not perfect, but enough to go on.'

Relieved, she closed the notebook and was just rising to her feet, ready to say goodnight, when he got up and came walking towards her, stretching widely.

'Now,' he said, standing over her. 'How about a nightcap?'

'Oh, Miles, I'm dead beat,' she began, but when she saw his face fall she reconsidered. 'All right. Just one.'

He went to the cupboard set in one of the bookshelves to take out a bottle of Scotch and a siphon bottle of soda and poured out their drinks. He came over and handed her a glass, then sank down in the easy-chair beside the table and took a long swallow.

'Ah,' he said contentedly. 'I needed that.'

He leaned his head back and closed his eyes again. As she watched him her heart went out to him. He looked as exhausted as she felt, his hair tousled from running his fingers through it, dark shadows under his eyes, the lines on his forehead etched more deeply. She was quite content to sit there quietly beside him, in a soothing silence, knowing somehow that he needed her presence.

Finally he opened his eyes and blinked them blearily at her, as though surprised to see her still sitting there.

'Well,' she said, getting up to leave, 'if you don't need me any more, I guess I'll get to bed.'

'I don't even want to think about that blasted book any more tonight. But don't go yet. Stay a while and talk to me. I'm still too wound up to sleep.'

'All right,' she said, and slowly resumed her seat.

He set his glass down, leaned back and crossed his arms behind his head. 'You know, I'm rather curious about you, Melissa,' he said at last.

'About me?' she said with a little laugh. 'I can't imagine why. I'm not very interesting.'

'Oh, but you are. For example, how does it happen that a young woman of your age and with your qualities is still unattached?'

He was leaning forward now, his penetrating grey eyes boring into hers, and Melissa shifted uncomfortably in her chair under the inquisition. He had touched on a subject she didn't like to discuss.

'Now,' he went on inexorably, 'I do recall that in one of our conversations on the ship you mentioned that there had been someone important to you in the past. What happened?'

She shrugged. 'I told you. It just didn't work out.'

'I know you did. But you didn't tell me why. Come on, Melissa.' His voice was low, insistent. 'Was he married? Gay? What was his name?'

'What does it matter to you?' she asked.

'I just don't believe it's healthy to keep such things bottled up inside. It would do you good to get it out in the open.'

'All right,' she said tartly. 'If you must know, I was in love once. And he left me because I wouldn't go to bed with him without some kind of commitment. Now, does that make you happy?'

'Oh, come on, Melissa,' he chided. 'Don't get temperamental on me. And isn't that a pretty archaic attitude towards love?'

As her irritation escalated, so did her nerve, making her bold. 'Well, what about you?' she said. 'I don't see any signs of an active love-life in this—this monk's cell of yours!'

He laughed drily. 'Oh, believe me, I'm far from a monk. But, as delectable as you females can be, I haven't found one yet who can get it through her head that I need to be left completely alone when I'm working.'

Somehow that word 'females' stuck in Melissa's craw. It made women sound like some species of brood mare. With great dignity, she raised herself to her full height, crossed her arms in front of her and gave him a pitying look.

'You know,' she said in a clear voice, 'if you weren't so smug I'd almost feel sorry for you.'

He opened his mouth, then snapped it shut, then opened it again. 'Now watch it, Melissa,' he said in a warning tone. 'Don't get carried away. You might just go too far.'

'And then what would you do?' she demanded. 'Fire me? Again?' She turned from him. 'Now, if you don't mind, I'm tired and I'm going to bed.'

She marched away from him, her back stiff as a ramrod, her hands clenched at her sides. Before she reached the door she heard his heavy footsteps crossing the room, then the tinkle of glass, the splash of soda, as he poured himself another drink.

The next day it was business as usual. They had just finished work late that afternoon, and Melissa was straightening the usual mess on her table. It had been a gruelling session and she was looking forward to a hot bath and early bedtime right after supper. She was just leaving when Miles called to her.

'By the way, an old friend of mine, David Lorimer, is coming over this evening for a meal and a game of chess. I'd like to have you join us for dinner in the dining-room.'

Startled, she turned to face him. 'I'd really rather eat in the kitchen with Maria and Pedro,' she said quickly.

'I know you would,' he replied. 'But I want you with us.'

'But why?'

'Well, for one thing I want you and David to meet. He's my lawyer, handles all my business affairs, and since you may have to deal with such things at some point you should get to know him.' He eyed her carefully. 'Also, I think you need some company. You're not a prisoner here, you know. When I said I wanted you generally available, I didn't mean that you couldn't have days off, see your friends, do whatever it is young girls do in their free time.' He laughed. 'Although old David isn't exactly the answer to a maiden's prayer, he's a good fellow, and I think you'll like him.'

For some reason that reference to 'young girls' rankled, not to mention the fact that he was once again trying to orchestrate her personal life as well as her working hours.

She gave him a cool look. 'Number one,' she said, 'I am not a "young girl", no matter what you think. And number two, I'm quite capable of deciding myself what to do with my free time.'

His eyes widened, then he scowled darkly. 'Well, you don't need to bite my head off. I was only thinking of you.'

Fat chance of *that*! she thought. 'Well, I'm sorry,' she said aloud. 'I didn't mean to sound snappish.' She began to shuffle papers together on her table, glancing at him out of the corner of her eye. 'One of us with temperament is quite enough,' she muttered under her breath.

For a moment she was sure he was going to blow, but instead he merely shrugged and made for the door. When he reached it he turned back. 'Have it your way,' he said. 'But I still expect you to show up in the diningroom for dinner with us. Seven o'clock sharp.'

CHAPTER SIX

IN THE end, Melissa did it, of course, not only because he'd virtually made it a command performance, but because she was curious to meet one of the few people he allowed into his personal life when he was working.

David Lorimer turned out to be a pleasant, stocky man with greying hair and a friendly, easy manner. When she got to the dining-room, at precisely seven o'clock, the two men were already there, standing by the large window that overlooked the garden, drinks in hand. When she stepped inside, Miles turned to her.

'Ah, Melissa,' he said. 'Let me introduce David Lorimer. David, my new secretary, Melissa Ryder.'

David took her hand in his. 'I'm very pleased to meet you, Melissa.' His pale blue eyes twinkled. 'Since you've managed to survive this long working for Miles, I assume you must be a young woman of sterling character.'

Melissa flicked a quick look at Miles, then smiled at David. 'I don't know about that,' she replied, deadpan, 'but it does seem to require a good deal of patience and fortitude.'

'Hold on, now,' Miles protested, frowning. 'It's not polite to dissect one's host like that. Especially before a meal.'

His tone was light, but Melissa could tell he was really rather annoyed. She and David exchanged a conspira-

torial smile just as Maria came in with their meal, and
they sat down to dinner.

After that the days and weeks passed quickly, and soon
it was the end of June, the beginning of summer, always
mild in Santa Barbara. Melissa had been living in Miles
Thatcher's house for almost two months, and she'd
become so accustomed to his routine by now that it
seemed she'd been there forever.

Except for David's visits, he had no other visitors when
he was working. Since he often referred to people he
knew, some of them quite famous, and places he'd been,
he was clearly a much more gregarious soul at heart when
he wasn't deeply involved in a book.

It did puzzle her, however, that he never referred to
a woman in his life, past or present. She knew he hadn't
lived a celibate life. He'd told her that much. Nor could
she forget that moonlight dance with him aboard ship.
She'd been certain then that he desired her, as any healthy
normal man desired a woman.

One bright summer day when she was in the kitchen
eating her lunch and watching Maria at the counter
pounding bread dough, she broached the subject.

'Maria,' she said between bites, 'how long have you
and Pedro been working for Miles?'

'Five years next month,' Maria replied promptly.

'Has he ever been married?'

Maria raised her eyes from her kneading and gave
Melissa a sharp look. 'Not that I know of,' she replied
flatly. 'At least not since I've been with him.'

Although it was instantly clear from Maria's tone that
she wasn't going to divulge any information about Miles's

personal life Melissa's curiosity got the better of her in the end and she plunged ahead.

'Well, he must have had some women in his life. I mean, he's an attractive man, after all, wealthy, successful. Women must fall all over themselves to get at him.'

'I don't know anything about it,' Maria replied, tight-lipped.

Well, so much for that, Melissa thought, getting up from her chair. She should have known better. 'It must be his rotten disposition,' she commented drily as she carried her dishes over to the counter.

To her surprise, Maria burst out laughing, and the two women exchanged a conspiratorial smile.

One sunny Friday afternoon a few weeks later, Melissa and Miles were in the study working—or trying to. Miles had spent a frustrating morning trying in vain to get past a sticky spot in the plotting of his book, and had ended the morning session sunk in gloom.

Things didn't improve at all after lunch, and while Miles paced restlessly back and forth in the room behind her Melissa sat staring dreamily out of the window, chin in hand, idly tapping her pencil on the table, waiting for inspiration to strike him.

'Will you please stop that infernal drumming?' she heard him bark suddenly.

Guiltily, she turned around. 'Sorry,' she said. 'I wasn't thinking.'

'Obviously,' was the curt retort.

She had to stifle a laugh at the comical sight he made. His dark hair was rumpled and standing on end, his features drawn and haggard, his grey eyes glazed over. He looked just like a man whose entire world had collapsed in ruins around him.

'I don't know how you expect me to concentrate when you're making that damned racket,' he said pettishly.

'Sorry,' she repeated, and this time she couldn't quite keep her mouth from twitching in amusement.

He put his hands on his hips and gave her a black look. 'Just what is it you find so funny?' he demanded. 'Please. Let me in on your little joke,' he went on with elaborate sarcasm. 'God knows I could use something to laugh at right about now.' He raked his fingers through his hair in sheer frustration.

With a heroic effort, Melissa wiped the incipient smile off her face and gave him a sympathetic look. He really was a pitiful sight. If that kind of agony was what it cost to be a great writer, she was grateful she was only a secretary.

'Listen, Miles,' she said, getting up and going over to him, 'I know I can't really understand what you're going through, and believe me I wouldn't dare presume to give you advice, but don't you think it might help clear your mind if you left it for a while?'

'And do what?' he snapped.

She shrugged. 'I don't know. Go out in the garden and smell the flowers. Drive to the beach. Take a swim in the pool. Anything! You're going to be a basket case if you keep on like this.'

He scowled darkly at her, ready to bite her head off again, she was certain, but then in the next instant he snapped it shut again. 'You're right,' he said at last. He thrust a tattered sheaf of yellow pages at her. 'Here,' he went on. 'See if you can piece this together with what you already have. I'm going for a walk.'

With that, he turned on his heel, threw his pen down on top of his desk and strode out of the room, leaving Melissa on her own to try to make sense of what he'd put on tape, what he'd dictated that morning and what she could decipher of the scrawling handwriting on the pages he'd given her.

After half an hour she had to give it up. There was no way she could get it all in proper sequence. Then, suddenly, from outside she heard a tremendous splash. She looked up, and through the window saw that Miles had just dived into the pool. As she watched him streaking from one end to the other, she had to smile a little to herself. He'd taken her advice after all.

It would be hopeless to go out and ask him for help. He'd only bark at her and tell her to use her own initiative. She'd just have to wait until he'd solved his problem. He was always more approachable then.

But on the other hand he'd also want the notes she was supposed to be transcribing. Either way, she couldn't win, and she could envisage another scene no matter what she did. Then suddenly a possible way out hit her. Miles kept an outline of the book somewhere in his desk. She'd typed it herself. If she could find it, she might at least be able to get the plot sequence right.

Very carefully, so as not to disturb anything, she went through the scattered piles of paper on top of the desk. In spite of the clutter he always knew instantly if one page was out of place. Finding nothing remotely helpful there, she started opening the drawers, still taking great pains to leave every scrap of paper exactly as she found it.

After a thorough search, there was still no sign of that outline. He must have taken it with him. She was just about to admit defeat and shut the last drawer when her eye was caught by a sheet of pink paper shoved down into the back behind a folder.

Pink? That wasn't like Miles. She bent down to take a closer look. Nor was the decidedly feminine hand-writing his. Melissa burned with curiosity. She took a quick glance out of the window. He was far enough away so that she'd have plenty of time.

Knowing she shouldn't, but unable to stop herself now, she reached into the drawer and pulled out the pink sheet, very cautiously, so as not to disturb anything else.

It was a letter, dated three months ago, which would put it right before the Mexico cruise.

Darling,
I know you told me not to write or call, but I can't believe you really meant it, not after all we've been to each other. How can you be so cruel? How can you simply forget that heavenly week in Paris, or the night you...

Here the page ended, and Melissa couldn't bring herself to turn it over. She already felt guilty enough. She had no business reading such an intimate letter.

Hastily she shoved it back in the drawer. But as she gave it one last look to make sure it was exactly the way she'd found it she noticed the signature at the bottom of the opposite side.

All my love, now and forever, Sandra.

She slammed the drawer shut and scurried back to her own desk. Her cheeks still burning, she sat there for a moment mulling over what she'd just seen. Poor Sandra, whoever she was. And how many others might there be? She offered up a heartfelt prayer of thanks that she'd had sense enough not to fall in love with him herself.

When she glanced out of the window again, Miles was just getting out of the pool. He stood at the edge for a moment, turned away from her, shaking the water off his dark hair. He made a fine figure in his dark swimming-trunks, hanging low on his lean hips now from the weight of the water, the muscles of his back and shoulders lean and sinewy, his legs long and straight.

Then she noticed that the skin of his back was much lighter than on his neck and arms, and it suddenly struck her that during the entire Mexican cruise she'd never seen him swim in the ship's pool, or even without a shirt on.

Putting a hand over her eyes to shade them from the sun, she leaned forward, peering more closely at him. There was something wrong with his back. As she squinted, focusing more narrowly on him, she saw that it seemed to be marked in a criss-cross pattern of some kind. It could only be scars!

Her head began to swim, and quickly she turned away. What could have happened to him to leave such permanent evidence? She recalled Frances's mention of his secret government work, and the photographs of such important people on the bookcase shelves, with their messages of gratitude.

Just then Miles came bursting into the room, wearing a terry-cloth robe, his head still wet. She'd been so absorbed in her thoughts that she hadn't heard him come in. Now, with a sinking heart, she realised she'd have to face him with the news that she'd made absolutely no headway whatsoever in the job he'd given her to do, and she didn't relish the thought.

She braced herself for the onslaught she knew was coming. 'Miles,' she began haltingly, 'I'm sorry, but I can't make any sense out of...'

'Never mind!' he said sharply, holding up a hand to stop her. 'Forget it. It doesn't matter.'

She stared at him. He was utterly transformed. The snappish monster who'd been on the edge of despair all day was now grinning broadly, the grey eyes alight with excitement.

He strode swiftly to her side, and before she knew what was happening had swept her up into his arms and was twirling her around in a kind of frenzied dance. Melissa was stunned. The man was a chameleon.

Finally he set her down, his hands still resting lightly on her shoulders. 'You were right!' he exclaimed happily. 'All it took was getting out of this damned room, into the fresh air, clearing my head.' He bent down and kissed her soundly, then cupped her face in his hands. 'I knew you'd be good for me, little Melissa,' he said softly, looking down into her eyes. 'With your quiet ways and good practical common sense, you're exactly what I need.'

Still bewildered at the dramatic change in him, she gave him a hesitant smile. 'Well, I'm glad,' she murmured.

'Now,' he said in a clipped voice, dropping his hands, 'half an hour's work should get the whole thing roughed out.' He sat down at his desk and started scribbling furiously on a blank yellow pad. 'We'll start that passage all over again, from scratch.'

She stood in the middle of the room gazing blankly at him. 'But what about the tapes you've dictated? All your notes?'

'Oh, throw them out,' he said with an expansive wave of his hand. 'It's all rubbish.' He looked up and frowned at her. 'Come on,' he said. 'Don't just stand there. I'll want you to take some of this down in shorthand.'

She turned then and went back to her table. 'Yes, sir,' she muttered under her breath on the way. 'Right away, sir.'

When he finally decided to quit it was more like two hours later than half an hour, and an intensive session it had been. By now Melissa's fingers were cramped and her mind so numb that she had serious doubts about ever being able to read the shorthand notes she'd so frantically taken down.

'My word,' he said, glancing at his watch, 'it's almost six o'clock! And David's coming for dinner tonight. It's time we stopped anyway. You can type that up tomorrow.' He peered closely at her. 'You *did* get it all down, I hope?'

'Oh, yes,' she assured him blithely, not at all sure, but too tired to get into a discussion of it with him at the moment.

'Good.' He bent his head over the yellow pad again. 'I'll just finish this up, but I won't need you any more today.'

Melissa got up and stretched her aching muscles, then started towards the door. As she passed by his desk, he glanced up at her.

'Wear something pretty tonight,' he said. 'I want to celebrate. In fact, I think I'll break out a bottle of champagne.'

She was about to ask him what difference it made what she wore, since both men ignored her throughout the entire meal anyway, but thought better of it at the last minute. He paid her salary, after all, and if part of her duties was to sit and listen to him talk to David she had no complaint.

'All right,' she said.

He nodded, then bent his head over his desk again, and Melissa, sighing deeply, left him to it.

That evening they were planning to eat on the terrace instead of in the dining-room. During the long summer days, it was light out until well past nine o'clock anyway, and as the back of the house faced west, with the setting sun in the background, it was ten o'clock before dusk really fell.

When Melissa stepped out on to the terrace, however, Miles was sitting there alone. He had just popped the cork on the champagne bottle and was pouring it out. She noticed then that there were only two glasses.

'Where's David?' she asked as she sat down. 'It's not like him to be late.'

'Oh, he's not coming,' Miles responded casually. 'He got tied up in court. We'll just have to celebrate alone.' He handed Melissa her wine. 'Cheers,' he said, raising his glass and tapping it lightly against hers. He took a healthy swallow, then gave her an appreciative look. 'You look very nice tonight.'

'Thank you,' she replied, a little taken aback. The Miles she knew wasn't usually so free with his compliments. He really was in a good mood.

She'd worn the sea-green dress she'd bought for the farewell ball on the ship, but this time had put a knitted white stole around her shoulders and fastened it in front with a pearl brooch. Not only could it get rather chilly after sunset, but the dress was far too bare for a dinner at home.

Home, she thought dreamily, as she settled back, sipping her champagne and gazing out at the rolling sea. Funny how she'd come to think of Miles's house as her home in just a few short months. As demanding and unreasonable as Miles could be, he'd never treated her like an outsider, but more as part of his family, a sister perhaps, along with Pedro and Maria.

He looked especially handsome tonight, wearing dark trousers and a white dress shirt open at the neck, the sleeves rolled up to reveal his strong forearms, lightly covered with silky black hair. He was freshly shaven, his deeply tanned face smooth, his dark hair brushed neatly. He was in an expansive mood, and spoke practically nonstop all through dinner, waving his fork in the air to make a point, laughing easily.

Just as they were finishing their meal, Maria appeared at the French doors leading into the house, a worried look on her normally placid face. She was waving her arms, obviously trying to attract Miles's attention, but his back was to her, so Melissa half rose from her chair, ready to go to her and see what she wanted. But Maria only threw up her hands and made straight for Miles.

'It's that Mrs Cooper,' she said with a loud sniff of disapproval. 'On the telephone.'

Miles's eyes flew open, his face hardened, and he scowled darkly. 'Sandra?' Maria nodded.

Melissa sat quietly in her chair, her hands folded in her lap, as the implications of that name dawned on her. Sandra! The pink letter she'd found in his desk! She was burning with curiosity, but kept her mouth clamped shut, waiting to see what Miles intended to do. Her call had obviously come as a total surprise to him. And a decidedly unpleasant one at that.

'Well, tell her I'm not home,' Miles said at last.

Maria shook her head. 'No,' she said, folding her arms across her ample bosom. 'She'll just keep calling. You better come.'

To make her point, she simply turned her back on him and plodded slowly back towards the house.

Miles darted one swift glance at Melissa, whose face remained impassive, then with a muttered, 'Excuse me,' he threw his napkin down on the table and strode into the house.

He wasn't gone long, and when he came back he just sat back down in his chair, picked up his fork, and without a word tucked back into the shrimp and avocado salad. Although the silence was a tense, uneasy one, Melissa wasn't going to let it spoil the wonderful meal, and kept on eating in silence.

Finally, he turned to her. 'Listen,' he said. 'I want to explain to you about Sandra. I mean, it's not what you think.'

'Miles, you don't have to explain anything to me about your personal life. You told me once it would be part of my job to protect your privacy. I don't need to understand.'

'But I want you to. I guess——' He broke off, flushing slightly. 'Well, I guess I value your good opinion. I just want you to know that whatever was between Sandra and me was over months ago. I'd made it clear from the beginning that I had no intention of making a permanent commitment to any woman, and she accepted that.'

'I see,' Melissa said. 'That makes it all right, then.'

He set his mouth in a thin line. 'Apparently you're not even going to try to understand.'

'Miles, would you rather I gave you a good dressing-down for treating this woman badly? I'm not suggesting that's what you did,' she added hastily. 'I just don't know what you want me to say.'

He only gave her another black look. 'Nothing,' he bit out at last. 'Not a thing.'

He pushed his chair back, rose to his feet and stood looking down at her for a moment. Then, muttering under his breath, something to do with people who had impossibly high standards, he marched back to the house. As she watched him go, Melissa had to smile. It did seem to matter to him what she thought, and that was something.

From then on, Miles made great progress on the book. Although he worked her hard, so that she fell into bed every night exhausted, she always got up again the next morning looking forward to the day's session. Not only was it fascinating to participate in a creative endeavour, but he was fun to be with these days, more playful, more chatty, much as he'd been on the voyage.

Then, after about two weeks of steady forward movement, Melissa began to recognise the signs of trouble ahead. There were long silences when he was dictating, his tapes were largely blank, and the yellow pages rarely contained more than a sentence or two scrawled on them.

One morning, just as they were finishing up another fruitless session, the telephone rang on Miles's desk. He reached for it and after a brisk hello listened for a moment, frowning. 'I'm sorry,' he said at last in a curt voice. 'I can't possibly.'

As Melissa watched him, wondering what was up, she could hear quite clearly a feminine voice coming from the other end. Could it be Sandra on the prowl again? With each second, his frown deepened, until finally he cut into the high-pitched gabble.

'Listen,' he said briskly. 'Don't you people understand plain English? It has always been my firm, unalterable policy never to make television appearances, and that's not going to change. I'm a writer, not a personality to be put on display. Whatever people need to know about me they can learn from my books.'

With a curt goodbye he hung up. Then, still glowering, he began to shuffle the papers on his desk. 'Now, where were we? Ah, yes, I want you to retype this page,' he said, handing her a sheet.

Throughout the entire telephone exchange, Melissa had only sat there, perfectly still, trying to make her face a blank to hide her disapproval. After all, it was none of her business.

'All right,' she said evenly, taking the paper from him.

He raised his head and glared at her. 'What's that supposed to mean?'

She widened her eyes in innocence. 'Nothing. I'm just agreeing with you.'

His gaze narrowed and he leaned forward. 'I know that look. Come on, out with it. What's wrong now?'

Melissa took a deep breath. 'All right, since you insist. I can't see what harm it would do to agree to that interview.' His face was like thunder now, and she hurried on before she lost her nerve altogether. 'I mean, I know how much your privacy means to you, but you're a famous person. I just think perhaps you owe it to the public that gave you that fame to let them see you once in a while, hear what you have to say. Besides, you seem to have hit another snag on the book. Maybe it would do you good to discuss it with an impartial observer.'

He opened his mouth, then snapped it shut and jumped to his feet. He went over to the window and stood there for a while, rubbing the back of his neck and gazing out into the garden.

Melissa sat in her chair, as quiet as a mouse, hardly daring to breathe, waiting for the axe to fall and wondering why in the world she'd even broached the subject in the first place. It was nothing to her whether he did the interview, and certainly not worth risking her cushy job.

Finally he turned around, folded his arms in front of him and leaned back against the window-seat. 'All right,' he said through his teeth. 'You may have a point. I'll

do it. But on the absolute provision that my personal
life will not be a subject for discussion. You can call that
woman back and tell her.'

'Me?' she said in alarm. 'Why me?'

'Well, it was your idea, wasn't it?' He ambled towards
her, a thin smile curled on his lips. 'Her name is Ann
Cameron. Her number is there on the desk some place.'
He glanced at his watch. 'Now I have a lunch date.'

With that he turned on his heel and left. Melissa stared
after him for several seconds, her mind a blank. Then,
with a sigh, she began to search for Ms Cameron's telephone number.

The night of the interview, Melissa, Maria and Pedro
sat in front of the television set watching and hanging
on every word. Melissa had extracted a solemn promise
from Ann Cameron to keep hands off all personal subjects, and so far it was all going quite well. Miles looked
wonderful, perfectly at ease, and charming the socks off
Ms Cameron as he discussed his book.

Then, suddenly, she leaned towards him and fixed him
with a gimlet eye. 'I understand from the grapevine, Mr
Thatcher, that at one time you were involved in secret
government work. Is that true?'

Miles's eyes glazed over. 'I'm afraid I can't discuss
that,' he said easily, brushing over it.

'Very well,' she said, smiling sweetly. 'But that *is* actually an answer, you know.'

Miles gave her a thin smile. 'That's *your* interpret-
ation, not mine,' he stated firmly.

She leaned even closer. 'Well, since you're uncomfortable with the subject, let's try something else.

For instance, I know you've never been married, but your name has been linked with several glamorous women. Would you care to comment on that?'

'Uh-oh,' Maria muttered under her breath.

Melissa tensed, waiting for the storm, praying Ms Cameron would have sense enough to back off. She searched Miles's face, but it had taken on that blank shut-in expression she knew so well, and she could sense that fireworks were imminent. Why in the world hadn't the blasted woman kept her promise?

But she persisted. 'Come on, now, Mr Thatcher,' she gushed. 'Don't be coy. Our viewers are interested in you as a person as well as a writer.'

Then, suddenly, Miles turned from her and smiled directly into the camera. 'Let me just say that I'm very grateful for the attention my books have received, and hope my next effort will be as well accepted.' Still smiling, he turned to the interviewer and nodded at her. 'And I want to thank you, Ms Cameron, for giving me this opportunity to discuss my work.'

Then he rose to his feet and calmly strolled off-camera, leaving Ann Cameron with her mouth hanging open, staring after him.

Maria and Pedro immediately burst into peals of delighted laughter, and Melissa had to smile. He'd carried it off perfectly, offending no one. He'd kept his temper in check and left Cameron holding the bag with at least five minutes of dead air time to fill.

Melissa stayed up waiting for him that night, but when he hadn't returned by eleven o'clock she decided to give up and go to bed. She only hoped he wouldn't blame her for what had happened.

Some time in the middle of the night, she was awakened by the sound of a light tapping on her bedroom door and someone calling her name in a low voice.

Groggily, she raised her head up off the pillow and glanced at the luminous dial of the bedside clock. It was past two o'clock in the morning! Maybe she'd been dreaming. Then it came again.

'Melissa.'

'Miles?' she called. 'Is that you?'

The door opened a crack, and in the glow of the hall light she could see him standing there, fully dressed, his hair dishevelled, his eyes wild.

'Can I come in?'

She pulled the covers up around her bare shoulders. 'All right,' she called back.

He stepped inside, leaving the door open, and came to sit down on the side of the bed. She could smell alcohol on his breath. He'd obviously stopped for a drink.

'Well, I hope you're satisfied,' he said. 'I knew that was going to happen.' Although his words were accusing, his tone was clearly joking.

'Well, then,' she replied, 'you were prepared, weren't you? That much was obvious.'

He chuckled then, deep in his throat, clearly very pleased with himself, and she wondered why. 'I must say, you don't seem very upset about that interview. I thought you'd be livid.'

'Oh, that,' he said, with a wave of his hand. 'That's not important. What is important is that I finally found the answer to my problem with the book.'

'Oh, Miles,' she said. 'That's wonderful. I'm so happy for you. What happened?'

'I don't know what happened,' he replied. 'After I left the television station I was just driving around, cursing the book, wishing I'd never started it in the first place, debating whether to chuck it and start all over or quit writing entirely, when all of a sudden the piece of the puzzle I've been searching for fell into place, and I knew exactly what I had to do.'

'But Miles,' she said, laughing, 'it always happens that way, doesn't it? You know the answer always comes eventually.'

He shook his head. 'I hear what you're saying, and in theory I agree with you, but at the time it just doesn't work. Every time I hit a real snag, it seems as though it's gone for good.'

She reached over and put a hand on his arm, looking up into his face, still drawn from his recent battle. 'Ah, but I know you better than that by now, Miles,' she said softly. 'It's in your nature to see all of life as a challenge, not a burden, and that includes your work.'

He gazed at her for a long time, and gradually the tension seemed to drain out of him. 'Bless you, Melissa,' he said at last in a low voice. 'You do understand, don't you? This book is the most ambitious project I've ever undertaken, and I want you to know that I couldn't have come this far without you.'

Melissa's heart swelled. At that moment she would have walked through flames for his sake. Here was one of the finest writers in the world, opening his heart to her, making himself vulnerable to her, relying on her help.

Their eyes met in silent communion, and slowly an electric tension started building up between them. When his gaze dropped lower, it suddenly occurred to her that in her excitement the covers had fallen away and all she had on was a flimsy summer nightdress.

But by then it was too late. His arms had come around her, and as he clung to her, the dark head buried in her shoulder, Melissa knew with a sinking heart that in spite of all her good intentions and fine resolutions she was at the cutting edge of falling hopelessly in love with him, probably had been from their first meeting on the ship.

CHAPTER SEVEN

IT WAS a magical moment, the balmy night air, the strong scent of the roses in the garden wafting in through the open window, the pale glow of the crescent moon. For that moment Melissa could almost believe they were back on the ship, only this time Miles had come into her cabin instead of leaving her at the door.

As she stroked the crisp, dark hair, she could feel his warm breath on her skin, the faint stubble rasping against it, and a surge of tenderness for him swept over her. He was so strong, yet so vulnerable, so clever, yet so foolish, and for the first time since they'd met she felt herself to be the one in control.

Yet that control was slipping fast. He had shifted his position slightly so that his lips were at the base of her neck, nuzzling, seeking. Her heart, which seemed to have stopped beating from the moment he took her in his arms, was now thudding heavily, and the sensations he was stirring within her clouded her mind so that she couldn't think straight.

Suddenly he raised his head up and gazed down into her eyes. 'Melissa,' he said softly. 'Oh, Melissa.'

She couldn't move, could scarcely breathe. The dear face, the glittering grey eyes, the large hands gripping her shoulders were the only reality, and she wanted this man as she'd never wanted anything before in her life.

127

And he wanted her! There was no mistaking that. But it was more than desire. He cared about her as a person. He'd shown it in a hundred little ways, and it made all the difference.

His head was bending down towards her now, and she closed her eyes, waiting breathlessly for his kiss. Then the mobile mouth was on hers at last, playing with her lips, brushing against them, keeping her in an agony of suspense, until finally his hold on her tightened, his mouth opened, deepening the kiss, and she felt herself being propelled backwards, his body pressing against hers until her head rested on the pillow.

It was then that she lost the last vestiges of control. She flung her arms around his neck, raking her hands up through his hair, ready to give him whatever he wanted from her. When one of his hands, large and warm, moved down to cover her breast, she moaned softly deep in her throat and arched her body up against his, longing for more.

He was lying down beside her now, his hands moving feverishly over her body, sliding the straps of her nightgown over her shoulders, then brushing sensuously across her bare breasts, his mouth still drinking greedily from hers. She slid her own hands up underneath his thin cotton shirt, running them over the bony ribcage, muscled chest and flat abdomen.

Then, suddenly, he left her. She opened her eyes and looked up at him. He had raised his head, his hands still braced on either side of her, and was staring wide-eyed out of the window, a look of fierce concentration on his face.

'Miles,' she whispered. 'What is it?'

He turned back and gazed down at her with something like horror in his eyes. 'Oh, God,' he breathed. 'What have I done?'

Abruptly he swung his legs over the side of the bed, braced his elbows on his knees and buried his head in his hands. Melissa sat up, really alarmed by now, and put out a tentative hand to touch his shoulder. Immediately he flinched away from her and jumped to his feet.

For a moment he didn't say anything, just stood there gazing down at her, his face in the shadows now so that she couldn't make out the expression on it. But from the uneven quality of his breathing she could tell that he was making an effort to get himself under control. Frantically she searched her mind for something to say to him, but by now she was so confused by his erratic behaviour that nothing made any sense to her.

Finally he spoke to her, his voice low, his tone flat. 'In a lifetime of fairly irresponsible moves,' he said, 'this just about beats them all.' He shook his head. 'I'm really sorry, Melissa. I guess I was so carried away with getting my plotting problem resolved that I lost my head. I know that's no excuse, but I can promise you it will never happen again.'

He continued to stand there, as though waiting for a reply, but the shock was too much for her. It had all happened so fast that she was still reeling from it. She heard his words, even understood them, but no matter how hard she tried she couldn't quite grasp their meaning.

Then, abruptly, he turned on his heel and stalked out of the room, closing the door quietly behind him. As she sat there in the bed listening to his footsteps going down the hall away from her, one fact stood out in her mind. He didn't want her after all. It was the only explanation. He said he'd been carried away by his excitement over the book. She was the nearest object to hand, but it could have been anyone. Even Maria, she thought bitterly.

She flopped her head back on the pillow. Still, for a while, he *had* wanted her. There was no mistaking that. Then something about her must have changed his mind. Tears of frustration and disappointment began to spill over, and she lay there, her eyes shut tight, fighting off the waves of self-pity that threatened to engulf her, trying to *think* her way out of the mess she found herself in.

Of course, she'd have to leave now. After what had happened tonight, there was no way she could stay in the same house with him, see him every day, knowing she couldn't have him. And no doubt he'd be glad to be rid of her, just as he was Sandra.

The next morning Melissa crept down the hall to the study before breakfast, hoping to beat Miles there so that she could straighten out her desk and pick up her few personal belongings before she left.

When she reached the door and peered inside, however, he was sitting there at his desk as usual, and before she could move he'd already spotted her. She braced herself for an unpleasant scene.

'Good morning,' he called to her cheerily. 'I'm glad to see you up so early. Now that I've seen the light I'd like to get the new sequence down while it's still fresh in my mind.'

She could only stare at him. He'd obviously been up working all night. He was wearing the same clothes, his dark hair was tousled, his face unshaven, his eyes red-rimmed. She started walking slowly towards her table, and as she passed by his desk he held up a sheaf of yellow paper, covered in his slashing black handwriting.

'There's more on your desk,' he said as she took it from him. 'I only hope you can decipher it all. Think you can get started on it now? Or have you had breakfast yet?' He glanced at his watch. 'Good lord!' he exclaimed. 'Is it seven-thirty already?'

She stood uncertainly beside his desk, holding the yellow sheets and wondering what to do. He had turned back to his work and was now busily filling yet another page. While she debated, she gazed down at his hands, one holding the pen, the other lying at the top of the pad. All she could think of was that those hands had moved over her body last night, and she flushed deeply at the memory.

Apparently he had forgotten the whole thing, or at least had no intention of raising the subject again. That might be all right for him, but it wasn't going to be quite so easy for her. He was her employer, it was his house. Her position was a little more awkward.

She cleared her throat loudly. 'Miles,' she said.

He finished the sentence he was writing, then turned to her, frowning. 'Yes? What is it?' He leaned back in his chair with a sigh. 'Listen, Melissa, if it's about last night, I've said all I'm going to on the subject. I made a mistake, but not an irreparable one, I hope, and the sensible thing now is to forget it.'

Better for whom? For him, of course. But, she had to admit, for her too, at least for the present, until she could make other plans. 'Then I take it you want me to stay,' she said.

His eyes flew open. 'Of course I want you to stay.' Then he grinned. 'You're the best secretary I've ever had. Surely you're not going to hold one slip, one error of judgement against me?' The smile broadened. 'I'm a temperamental artist, remember? You have to make allowances for me.' Then he sobered. 'But I meant it when I said it wouldn't happen again. You don't have to worry about that.'

Melissa was torn between thanking him and hitting him. Although it was in her best interest to stay on at the moment, it irritated her that he could dismiss the whole episode so blithely when she'd been agonising over it practically the whole night.

'Well, if you don't mind,' she said tartly at last, 'I'm going to have breakfast before I start.'

'Fine,' he said. 'You do that.' Then he turned from her, snatched up his pen, and bent his head over his work again.

Miraculously, they settled back into their old routine. The plotting of the book continued to progress well, with no more snags, and the matter was never referred to again.

In time, Melissa even began to wonder if it hadn't been a dream. Sometimes, watching him unawares when he was working or talking to David at dinner or laughing at some joke, she would remember how it had felt to be in his arms, but she quickly dismissed those thoughts.

She really did like working for him, and it was probably better to be his valued secretary than his mistress anyway.

Because of the more orderly schedule, she now had more free time of her own, time she could count on. This was all to the good, except that she found herself using that time mooning around the house and brooding about Miles when he was gone, wondering where he went, what he was doing, and, most of all, whom he was doing it with.

After a few weeks of this, it dawned on her that what she needed was more life of her own. She'd been sequestered here in the house with Miles, involved in *his* interests, seeing *his* friend, catering to *his* needs, for months now. It was time she looked up a few of her own friends.

One evening, then, in late August after Miles had left the house, she went into the study to call Frances. Monterey wasn't that far away. Surely they could meet somewhere in between.

Frances herself answered after the second ring, and when Melissa heard the familiar voice she felt a sudden rush of affection for the pleasant older woman who'd been so kind to her on the cruise.

'Frances, this is Melissa Ryder. Remember? We met on the trip to Mexico.'

'Melissa!' she cried, obviously pleased. 'It's so good to hear from you. Of course I remember you. In fact, I tried to call you weeks ago—months, it is now—but they said your telephone had been disconnected. What in the world happened to you?' She laughed. 'I was about to call in a private detective to hunt you down.'

'I'm sorry, Frances. It was wrong of me just to disappear like that, but when we got back—in fact that very day—I started a new job and have been so busy ever since that I haven't had a minute even to think of anything else.'

'Well, it sounds interesting anyway. What kind of job?'

Melissa hesitated. Surely Miles couldn't object to anyone knowing that she worked for him. 'Well, as a matter of fact, I'm working as secretary to Miles Thatcher.'

For a moment there was utter silence on the line. Then Frances expelled a deep breath. 'No!' she said in a hushed voice. 'I don't believe it. How in the world did that come about?'

'On the last day of the trip he simply came to my cabin and asked me if I wanted to work for him. If you recall, I'd just lost my old job, and since he lived right here in Santa Barbara it seemed like a gift from heaven.'

'Well, for the land's sake! Of all things!' Frances spluttered, still obviously astounded at the news.

Melissa had to laugh. 'Just imagine how surprised I was when he sprang it on me.'

'Well, all I can say is, lucky you! What a plum that is! You must have made quite an impression on him. So tell me, what's it like working for a genius? Do you enjoy it?'

'For the most part, yes. Although it does have its drawbacks. Artistic temperament, you know. He's almost paranoid about his privacy, so please don't ask me any questions about him.'

'I wouldn't dream of it, my dear,' Frances replied loftily, which they both knew was a patent lie. 'Now, when can we get together? Do you have any free time? I'd love to have you come and stay with me for a while in Monterey. It's so lovely here this time of year, and I have a nice guest bedroom you could use.'

'I don't know about that,' Melissa replied slowly. 'I may only be able to get away for the day. I'll look into it and let you know. Are you free in the next few weeks?'

'Perfectly. Oh, and you'd better give me your number in case I need to call you.'

Melissa did so, adding, 'Since it's Miles's private unlisted number, you'd better not give it out to anyone else.'

'My dear, I wouldn't dream of it. Although that reminds me. Your friend Jack has called me a few times to see if I'd heard from you. Apparently he's been trying to get in touch with you, too. Really, Melissa, it was too bad of you just to vanish that way.'

'Jack?'

'You know, the handsome young Viking from the cruise.'

'Of course.' Melissa flushed with pleasure. How could she forget? What surprised her was that he hadn't forgotten her.

'Well?' Frances was asking. 'Would it be all right to give him your number if he calls again?'

'Yes. Of course.' It was her home, too. If Miles didn't like it he could get her a telephone of her own.

'Well, it was lovely to hear from you, Melissa, and I'll look forward to seeing you soon. Come when you can and stay as long as you like.'

The next afternoon, after they'd finished for the day and Melissa had tidied her table, she went over to Miles's desk and stood there waiting while he finished the last correction.

He looked up at her. 'Yes?'

'I was just wondering, Miles, now that the work on the book seems to be settling down, if I couldn't start taking some time off.'

He dropped his pen and leaned back in his chair, gazing up at her. 'What for?'

'Well, I do have a personal life, after all,' she replied tartly. 'Or I used to, at any rate.'

'I told you once you weren't a prisoner here. What did you have in mind?'

'I'd like two or three days. You see, a friend of mine has invited me——'

Just then the telephone rang on his desk. He reached for it, listened for a moment, frowning, then handed it to Melissa. 'Here,' he said, 'it's for you.'

'For me?' she asked, surprised as she took it from him.

'Well, at last!' a man's voice said. 'I've been trying to get hold of you for ages. It's Jack. You remember me, don't you? From the cruise? I just happened to call Frances again last night to see if she'd heard from you, and she gave me your number. Quite a coincidence, isn't it?'

'Yes,' she replied. 'It is. It's wonderful to hear from you, Jack. How have you been?'

'Well, I've given up the great acting career.'

'Oh, I'm sorry. What are you doing?'

'Actually, I've had a few modelling jobs. It pays well, and I can pretty well work when I please.'

All the while they spoke, Melissa was uncomfortably aware that Miles was sitting quite firmly in his chair, as though rooted to it, listening to every word. You'd think, she grumbled to herself, he'd have the courtesy to leave the room, give her some privacy.

'Anyway,' Jack was going on, 'I'd sure like to see you again. Frances said you might be going up to Monterey to spend some time with her. I have friends in Carmel I could stay with. Maybe we could drive up together some weekend soon.'

'That would be lovely, Jack,' she replied, cooing sweetly for Miles's benefit. 'I'll have to find out first what weekend I could get away.' She gave Miles a swift covert glance and was pleased to see his face darken in annoyance.

'Sure,' Jack said. 'Any time. In the meantime, how about dinner this Saturday? Maybe I could get some of the old gang together and make a day of it. We could have a reunion party.'

'Oh, I'd love that.'

'Great. How about if I pick you up around noon?'

'Sounds good.' She gave him directions to the house then, and they said goodbye.

When she reached in front of Miles to replace the receiver, he didn't utter a word, nor did she look at him, but the unmistakable vibrations of hostility emanating from his still form spoke louder than any words.

'Well!' he said at last, just as she started to leave.

She turned to face him. He was sitting just as she'd left him, leaning back in his chair, his arms crossed over his chest, glowering darkly at her. 'Well what?' she asked innocently.

'I must say, Melissa, that I'm surprised at you.'

She goggled at him. 'At me? Why? What have I done?'

He leapt out of his chair and began pacing the room, coming to a halt at her side and pointing an accusing finger at her. 'Going off with that—that——' He shook his head. 'Words fail me.'

'Well, I'm sorry,' she said tartly. 'I didn't mean to offend your delicate moral sensibilities. Besides,' she went on before he could get a word in, 'I'm not "going off" with anyone. At least not the way you mean it.'

'Hah!' was all he said.

'Just what does that mean?' she demanded.

'Perhaps you've forgotten,' he went on in a maddening tone, 'that I had to rescue you, not once, but twice, from that...' He shook his head as words obviously failed him again.

Fun was fun, but by now she was growing seriously annoyed. They stood there glaring at each other for several seconds. Melissa hardly trusted herself to speak, but finally she put her hands on her hips and thrust her face up close to his.

'You've got some nerve,' she said in a low voice throbbing with emotion, 'criticising my perfectly innocent actions considering the shambles you've made of *your* love-life. I don't know why I have to explain anything at all to you, but if I can't make a simple date with a man without your blowing it up into the scandal of the century maybe it's time I left.'

His eyes flew open at that, and he seemed seriously alarmed. Then, with a noise of disgust deep in his throat, he made a sweeping gesture with his hand. 'All right,' he said loftily. 'Have it your way. If you want to waste your time on layabout surfers, pretty boys who have nothing to offer but their youth and good looks, go ahead. It's your funeral.' He pointed at her again. 'But I don't want a lot of noisy youths and giggling girls cluttering up my house.'

'Very well,' she announced stoutly. 'I'll call Jack and tell him I'll have to meet him in town because I'm not allowed to have visitors here.'

'I didn't say that!' he barked. 'Of course you can have visitors. Just try to keep the volume down when I'm working.'

'Yes, sir,' she replied sweetly. 'I'll do that.'

For the next few days as they worked together Melissa and Miles circled wearily around each other, like a cat and a dog on the brink of open warfare. They were silent for the most part, but when they had to speak it was always with elaborate politeness.

For the life of her, Melissa couldn't figure out what had set him off that way. Surely he couldn't object to her having some social life of her own. Lord knew she'd spent every waking moment at his beck and call for months now, and had earned a reprieve once in a while. Of course, he detested Jack, but that was her affair, not his. He wasn't her father, after all. Hardly that, after the scene in her bedroom.

Occasionally she would catch him looking at her with a strange fixated stare that was half irritated, half puzzled, and the fleeting thought came to her that he was acting very much like a jealous lover over the whole affair. But that couldn't be, and she always quickly dismissed it as an idle fantasy, out of the question.

She'd meant to buy a new dress for the date with Jack, but Miles kept her so busy all day Thursday and Friday that she didn't have a free moment to do any shopping.

The green party dress would have to do. Luckily Saturday
dawned bright and sunny, and with a light sweater and
low-heeled sandals she'd be prepared for anything.

On Saturday Jack arrived promptly at noon, driving
a sleek red convertible. Melissa was waiting for him
outside on the wide veranda. On no account did she want
Miles anywhere within shouting distance. She'd been
positive up until the last minute that he'd dream up some
emergency with the book to keep her from going, but
instead he hadn't worked at all that day.

To her dismay, Jack gave the horn two good sharp
blasts when he saw her. Quickly she gathered up her
handbag and ran to the car. He'd leaned across the seat
to open the door for her, a broad grin on his handsome
face. He looked wonderful, deeply tanned, white teeth
flashing, his blond hair gleaming in the sunshine.

'Gosh, it's great to see you, Melissa!' he called. 'Hop
in.'

'It's good to see you, too, Jack,' she said, getting
inside. 'You look as though you've been spending a lot
of time in the sun.'

'Ah, the surf's been up at Malibu,' he explained.

Melissa suppressed a giggle, recalling Miles's comment
about layabout surfers. 'Yes, I can tell.'

He put the car in gear and they shot off down the
drive, the tyres squealing at every curve. As they passed
by the house, she glanced at the window of the study,
and for a moment, before they sped past it, she was
certain she could see a dark, brooding shape standing
there staring out at them.

It was almost midnight when Jack drove her home.
She half expected Miles, ever on the alert for her virtue,

to be waiting up for her, but except for the lights burning on the veranda by the front door the house was totally dark and silent as the grave.

'Thanks for the lovely day, Jack,' she said when he stopped the car in front of the house. 'I had a wonderful time.'

'So did I,' he replied. 'We'll have to do it again soon.'

It had been an almost perfect day. Friends of Jack's had a boat docked at the marina, and several of the crowd from the cruise had met them there, including Terry. After a marvellous seafood lunch at a nearby restaurant, they'd spent the afternoon on the boat, cruising around the sheltered bay, swimming, sunbathing, playing silly card games or just listening to pop music.

They'd had dinner at a popular Mexican restaurant, eating outside on the terrace and listening to the strains of a mariachi band, all reminiscent of the trip to Mexico. To Melissa's great relief, Jack had paced his drinking sparingly, and although he was in his usual fine form, the perennial life of the party, he managed to stay quite sober the entire day.

After switching off the engine, he turned to her and draped an arm casually around her shoulders. 'I hope you noticed how well I behaved myself today,' he said, half teasing, half serious.

'As a matter of fact, I did.' She laughed. 'I hope it didn't spoil your day.'

'Not at all. In fact, I'm a reformed character now. I mean, you miss all the fun of a party when you're half unconscious—or sick. Besides, I'll be thirty on my next birthday, and it's time I became a more responsible citizen.'

She smiled at him, and in the glow of the lamps on the veranda their eyes met. He moved a little closer, tightening his hold on her, and put his other hand on her face.

'I really like you, Melissa,' he said softly. 'Have done, right from the start. There's something so real about you, so serious. You seem to settle me down, bring out the best in me.'

'Why, Jack!' she said. 'What a nice thing to say.'

She knew he was going to kiss her, and when his lips did come down on hers she closed her eyes. It was a sweet kiss, and she quite enjoyed it, but no bells rang, her pulse didn't quicken, even when his mouth became more urgent and seeking.

When he drew away from her she smiled at him again. He really was a dear boy, but that was how he seemed to her—a boy; at least compared to—— She looked away, biting her lip, suddenly aware of the direction her thoughts were leading her.

'I'd better go in now,' she said.

He walked with her to the door. 'I'll call you the next time I can get away,' he said.

'I'll look forward to it,' she replied, meaning it.

He kissed her again, briefly, saw her safely inside, then went back to the car and drove off.

The next day was Sunday, and Melissa got up later than usual. There was no sign of Miles, so after a leisurely breakfast she went down the hall to the study to see if he might be working.

She found him there, bent over his desk as usual, pen in hand. 'Good morning,' she said, stepping inside. 'I see you're already hard at it. Sorry I'm a little late, but I wasn't sure you'd want to work today.'

After a moment, he raised his head, leaned back in his chair and gave her a long searching look. Melissa braced herself for more snarling sarcasm about her date with Jack and the inevitable inquisition, but instead, to her surprise, he gave her a warm, almost paternal smile.

'Have a good time yesterday?' he asked pleasantly.

'Yes,' she said, still wary. 'I did.'

'That's good. I hope you don't mind working for a few hours today. I'm so close to the end now that I hate to leave it.'

'Not at all,' she said. Still confused, she walked slowly over to her table to get a pad and pencil.

From then on he continued to treat her with elaborate courtesy. He seemed to be putting a cool distance between them, almost as though he was going out of his way to prove he didn't care what she did in her own time. Although it was a relief not to have to defend herself against his criticisms, now that he was doing as she'd asked and leaving her personal life alone she rather missed that old concern, in spite of the high-handed way he had of showing it.

One Friday afternoon they were working in the study as usual. She'd been transcribing the tapes he'd dictated the night before, while he was bent over his desk, scribbling away.

Finally he pushed back his chair, snatched up a handful of yellow sheets and carried them over to her desk. 'There!' he said, throwing them down on the table beside her typewriter. 'It's done!'

She looked up at him. He was grinning from ear to ear, a bright gleam of triumph in his silvery eyes, intense satisfaction written all over his face.

'Why, that's wonderful, Miles!' she exclaimed, returning his smile. 'Congratulations.'

He rubbed his hands together, eyes sparkling. 'I think this calls for a celebration, a real party.'

She had to smile. He was like a small boy who had just received his heart's desire from Santa Claus. 'Sounds great to me,' she replied.

'You've been such a help to me,' he went on in the same euphoric mood, 'that I intend giving you a hefty rise in salary.' He paused for a moment and stared at her, frowning. 'Just do me one favour. Spend at least part of it on a new outfit for the party. As far as I can tell you haven't had a new dress since I've known you.' He shook his head. 'Modesty becomes you, Melissa, but if you're going out on the town with me I don't want people to think I pay my secretary poverty-level wages and keep you in rags.'

Before she could utter a word, he turned on his heel and strode jauntily out of the room, whistling loudly as he went. She sat there for several moments staring after him, really hurt at his criticism of her clothes. Then she glanced down at her old blue cotton shirtwaister and was forced to admit he did have a point. She really did look rather shabby.

'By gum,' she muttered to herself at last, 'I'll show him!'

CHAPTER EIGHT

Two weeks later, on a Saturday night, Melissa stood before her bedroom mirror for one last quick glance. She'd just heard David's car come up the drive, and it was time to leave for the party.

Although she was pleased with the results of her make-over, her heart quailed now at the dramatic change in her appearance. Perhaps she'd overdone it. The upswept hairstyle suited her fine-boned features, but made her look older, more sophisticated, and the cherry-red dress with the tiny straps was cut just a little too low for comfort. She'd have to be very careful bending over.

What worried her most was the brand-new high-heeled sandals. She wasn't used to walking in those slim spikes, and was terrified she'd trip. What had seemed like such a brilliant scheme a few weeks ago when Miles made the snide comment about her clothes now seemed like a childish gesture that would only make her look ridiculous.

However, it was too late to back out now. The doorbell had just rung and she could hear the low-pitched rumble of David's voice as Maria let him in. Taking a deep breath, she squared her shoulders and headed down the hall to meet him, stepping very carefully over the carpet in her new high heels.

'Hello, David,' she said. 'I'm sorry you got stuck having to come to pick me up. I could just as easily have driven myself.'

He was standing there goggling at her. 'Melissa!' he said, walking towards her and holding out his hands. 'You look——' He broke off, and shook his head. 'Words fail me.'

She gave him a shaky smile and raised her chin. 'I hope that doesn't mean you disapprove.'

His pale blue eyes swept her up and down. 'Oh, no,' he said with feeling. 'Certainly not that. I guess I just never realised what a gorgeous creature lurked beneath the efficient secretary. And as for coming to pick you up, it's my pleasure.'

At first Miles had planned to have his party at home, but as the guest list had grown he'd decided it would be too much trouble for Maria, and, since she wouldn't hear of a caterer in her kitchen, he'd ended up booking a private room in the poshest local hotel.

To Melissa's surprise, he had insisted on making all the arrangements himself. Except for a few minor chores he'd asked her to perform, like addressing invitations and noting acceptances, he'd taken care of every minute detail, even to choosing the food and wine.

David came up beside her now and took her by the arm. 'Well, then, if you're all ready, shall we go?'

On the short drive to the hotel they chatted about the guests Miles had invited, a long list which included a congressman, a famous opera singer, two film stars, and several of Santa Barbara's more prominent citizens, not to mention two or three other writers. In fact, it was quite an impressive roster, and the closer they came, the more nervous Melissa became. It was exactly the kind of social occasion where she felt the most uncomfortable and inept, and she dreaded having to enter into what would no doubt be brilliant conversation, to make small talk with people she didn't even know.

As though sensing her unease, David skilfully changed the subject. 'So, Melissa,' he said. 'How do you like working for Miles by now?' He flashed her a smile. 'Since you've lasted over four months, I assume you must be satisfying him, but how about you?'

'Well,' she replied cautiously, 'it does have its ups and downs, but it's certainly the most interesting job I've ever had.' She paused for a moment. 'You've known Miles for a long time, haven't you, David?'

'Oh, lord, yes. Donkey's ages.'

'I've been wondering about those scars on his back. I noticed them one day when he was out swimming.'

He didn't say anything for a long time, and Melissa was beginning to regret having asked him. 'I'm sorry, David,' she said. 'I didn't mean to pry, and I certainly would never ask you to break any confidences.'

'Well,' he said slowly at last, 'you know how Miles is about his past. However, it's a matter of public record that he was a POW in Vietnam for a time, so I'm not really betraying any confidence by telling you that.'

'Thanks, David,' she said. 'Poor Miles. An experience like that must have left more scars than the ones on his body.'

He turned briefly to give her a warm smile. 'You're quite a girl, Melissa,' he said. 'In fact, you're probably the best thing that's happened to Miles in a long time.'

This surprised her. As far as she could gather, David barely knew she existed, except as part of the furniture, much less that he'd taken the trouble to analyse her relationship with Miles.

'I've often thought,' he went on, 'just how bored you must be on the nights I come to dinner. It can't be much fun for you to sit there listening to our conversation. I've tried to include you from time to time, but you know what Miles is when he gets started on one of his pet topics.'

'I'm not in the least bored,' Melissa said firmly. 'I enjoy listening to you. I'm not much of a talker myself anyway, and since I only had enough education to earn a living I'm anxious to learn. Listening to you and Miles talk is like going to school.' She laughed. 'Although I'm not sure just how much of it I grasp. I do try to read up on it later, though.'

'That's probably the best way to learn anyway,' he said with a nod of approval. 'What you find out on your own is usually what sticks the longest.'

They had arrived at the hotel now, and as David pulled into the curving drive Melissa felt her nerves start to twang again. The uniformed valet came rushing out to open her door, and they went inside the lobby. As they approached the room Miles had reserved, through the open door came the sounds of loud conversation, laughter, soft music in the background, and the clink of glasses.

She stopped short, suddenly panicked, and looked up at David. He gave her a swift questioning glance. Then, with a reassuring smile, he tucked her arm firmly under his and held it to his side.

'There's not a thing in the world for you to worry about, Melissa,' he said in a low, comforting voice. 'You look perfectly lovely, a match for any woman in the place. Just be yourself.' He smiled. 'Miles may seem a little insensitive at times, but, believe me, he'd never put you in a position where his friends might embarrass you. Besides, I know most of them, and even though a few might be famous they're only human beings, just like you and me. OK?'

She nodded and squeezed his arm. 'Thanks, David. It'll be all right.'

Inside there were what seemed like hundreds of people milling around, and they all seemed to know each other. Actually, she knew from the guest list that there weren't more than twenty. It just seemed like more because of all the talking, shouting and laughing.

The hotel was located on a bluff overlooking the harbour, and the room Miles had chosen commanded a striking view. In front of the window was a long table covered with snowy white linen, delicate china, fragile crystal and gleaming silverware. Soft music drifted in through the open door from the adjoining dance-floor, and it all seemed more like a rather opulent private home than a public dining-room. On one wall there was even a fireplace that looked as though it had never been used.

Melissa scanned the crowd, searching for Miles, but before she could spot him a man came sauntering up to David, hand outstretched, blocking her view. He was young and good-looking, dressed formally, and there was something vaguely familiar about him.

'Melissa,' David said, after greeting him, 'let me introduce Tony Fairchild, another writer. I'm sure you've heard of him.'

Of course she recognised the name immediately, and the face too, from the dust jackets on his books, hard-boiled detective stories that were immensely popular.

Flustered, she held out her hand. 'How do you do, Mr Fairchild? I've enjoyed your books very much.'

'Tony, please,' he said. He laughed. 'Afraid I'm not in Thatcher's class, but thanks anyway.' His eyes flicked over her in open appraisal. 'So you're the famous secretary,' he went on. 'I'd heard how efficient you were, but I wouldn't have credited old Miles for having such good taste in other respects.'

When his gaze settled on the low neckline of her red dress, Melissa flushed deeply. Famous secretary? She had no idea any of Miles's friends even knew she existed. When he was working, he erected such rigid barriers against the outside world that she was surprised now to realise that he must have kept in contact with some of them for news of her presence to leak out.

Someone called Tony's name, and before turning away he flashed her a suggestive look. 'I'll see *you* later,' he said.

When he was gone, out of her line of vision, she finally spotted Miles. He was standing by the fireplace, one elbow braced on the mantelpiece, drink in hand, talking to two women, who were laughing, apparently over a story he was telling.

He was looking especially handsome tonight in his dark suit, crisp white shirt and tie. She'd never seen him so animated. His silvery eyes were sparkling, the colour in his face was high, and he was gesturing with his hands to illustrate his story.

She recognised one of the women as a well-known actress, the other a model she'd seen in magazine advertisements. Both were beautifully turned-out, wearing expensive gowns and loaded with jewellery, and both gazing up at Miles with rapt attention.

Then, just as he finished his story, still laughing, he raised his head, and before Melissa could turn away their eyes met. Suddenly the laughter faded on his lips and he simply stood there gazing at her over the heads of the two women. Nervous at being caught staring at him, she averted her eyes, but not before she'd seen him come walking slowly towards her.

'Well, Miles,' she heard David say, 'this is quite a party you've put on. Good wine, interesting conversation, beautiful women. Speaking of which, what do you think of our Melissa? Quite a transformation, wouldn't you say?'

With a shy smile, Melissa turned to Miles, only to see that all traces of his former merriment had vanished. If looks could kill she'd be lying dead at his feet. Her face fell. She raised a hand to her hair and gave him a nervous look, but by then a mask had fallen over his features.

'Yes,' he replied. 'Quite a change.' He raised his drink and finished what was left of it in one long swallow. 'It's about time they were serving dinner.' He turned to her. 'Melissa, would you see that the guests are seated in their proper places?'

'But I don't even know them,' she objected.

'There are name-cards at each place.' His eyes flicked at David. 'And I'm sure David will be glad to help you identify them.'

When they finally got everyone seated, the waiters started serving dinner. Luckily Melissa was seated next to David, and her other dinner partner, one of the congressmen, was so busy trying to impress the actress on his other side that she didn't have to make conversation with him at all.

Miles, holding court at the head of the table, was still in high spirits, and Melissa was happy to see him so relaxed. She'd almost forgotten how entertaining he could be when he tried. He was amusing, too, with a dry wit that poked fun at just about every sacred cow under the sun.

Since he'd ordered dinner beforehand she didn't have to choose from an elaborate menu, and while in most cases she had no idea what she was eating it all tasted marvellous. He'd also chosen the various wines to go with each course, and by the time the meal was over all the guests were feeling rather tipsy.

After coffee and dessert had been served, the guests began to rise and straggle out towards the dance-floor, and before long Miles and David and Melissa were left at the table. While the two men chatted idly, drinking brandy, Melissa sat between them, happily stuffing the last delicious bite of crêpes Suzette into her already overloaded stomach.

Suddenly the orchestra in the next room broke into a lively tango, and she heard Miles raise his voice. 'David, did I ever tell you about Melissa's star turn in the ballroom on the Mexican cruise?'

Startled, she darted him a swift look. 'Oh, Miles,' she protested. 'It was hardly that.'

Ignoring her, he launched into a vivid description of the tango she and Jack had danced the night of the farewell party, including the applause at the end of it. By the time he'd finished, her cheeks were burning, but his tone was so good-natured and he had such a colourful way of telling a story that she couldn't possibly take offence.

They were still laughing over the episode when David suddenly scraped his chair back and rose to his feet, bowing deeply to her.

'Since you're an expert, would you do me the honour? My tango is a little rusty, but maybe you can give me a few pointers.'

Melissa giggled. 'Oh, David, I'm so stuffed I don't think I could move.'

He only smiled and held out a hand. 'Come on. The exercise will do you good. Besides, it'll boost my ego no end to be seen dancing with the loveliest woman in the place.'

'Well, how can I resist that?' she said, rising to her feet.

'Excuse us, Miles?' David asked.

'Certainly,' was the clipped reply, and off they went. David turned out to be quite a good dancer, and after the tango they danced another full set. Then Tony Fairchild cut in, but since he'd had more than his share of wine he wasn't much of a partner. Occasionally she would notice Miles's dark head as he danced by with one after another of the women guests. He was still animated and obviously enjoying himself, but as she danced one last set with David he seemed to have disappeared.

They finally started back into the dining-room, and as they went David put both hands on her waist to guide her, holding her a little more tightly, she thought, than was really necessary, but she was in such high spirits, from the wine, the fine dinner and the fun of dancing again, that she rather enjoyed the sensation.

It was quite late by now, and most of the guests had left. When they arrived back in the dining-room, Miles was sitting at the table. But he wasn't alone. The lovely model he'd been speaking to earlier was sitting next to him, quite close, her long black hair almost brushing his face. The black dress she had on was both strapless and backless, and cut so low that it left very little to the imagination what was beneath it. And I worried about *my* dress being too suggestive, Melissa thought indignantly as she made for her seat.

Just then David leaned down to put his mouth at her ear. 'Uh-oh,' he murmured. 'Looks as though there might be fireworks ahead.'

Melissa swivelled her head around to look up at him. There was a knowing grin on his face, a twinkle in his eyes. 'What do you mean?' she asked.

'The brunette,' he replied. 'Her name is Sandra Cooper, an old flame. And one that burned out long ago. Although it seems she might have other ideas, wouldn't you say?'

Aha! Melissa thought. The famous Sandra of the pink letter in Miles's desk! She took a closer look. The expression on Miles's face was one that was all too familiar to her, set and closed-in, giving away nothing, while the brunette, who seemed to be doing most of the talking, was fixing him with a determined look that almost vibrated with passionate intensity.

After seating Melissa carefully, David excused himself. 'I'll be right back, though,' he added. Then, totally out of character, he gave her bare shoulders a squeeze. 'Don't go away.'

Still puzzling over the unexpected gesture, Melissa glanced up the table at Miles and Sandra. They were still speaking in low, hushed voices, and, although she couldn't make out any of the words, from the tension that virtually sizzled between them it was clearly an argument.

Melissa felt quite awkward. She didn't know whether to stay or go. Actually, she might as well not even have been there for all the attention they paid to her. She had just about made up her mind to leave when Sandra rose abruptly to her feet and stood looking down at Miles.

'Well, if that's the way you feel about it,' she said angrily, 'I might as well go.' Then she turned on her heel and stalked off.

When she was gone, Miles took a last swig of his brandy then carefully placed the glass back on the table, his face sombre, as though deep in thought.

Then his glance settled on Melissa. 'Well,' he said, 'how was the dancing?' He was smiling now, but it seemed forced.

'Oh, it was great fun,' she replied brightly. 'David's a wonderful dancer.'

Miles nodded abstractedly, then rose slowly to his feet. 'Well, then, if you've had enough, perhaps it's time to leave. Most of the others have gone, and I am rather tired. Unless, of course, you and David would rather stay without me.'

'Oh, no,' Melissa said, getting up quickly. 'I'm ready to leave whenever you are.' She smiled at him. 'It was a marvellous party, Miles. A great success. And I've had such a good time.'

'Good,' he said absently. 'I'm glad you enjoyed it.'

David came back just then, and when he saw Miles and Melissa standing there alone, obviously getting ready to leave, his face fell. 'Not going already?' he said.

'I think so,' Miles replied. He glanced at Melissa. 'Are you certain you don't want to stay? I'm sure David will be happy to drive you home.

'Of course,' David put in quickly. 'Stay and have one last dance with me, Melissa.'

'No,' she said. 'No, thanks, David. I'm rather tired.'

The waiter came scurrying up to Miles just then with the bill. Miles hastily scrawled his signature on it, and they left.

The drive home was largely a silent one. Melissa made a few half-hearted attempts to discuss the party, but Miles seemed so abstracted that she didn't get much change out of him.

Of course he was tired, but she was almost certain something else was troubling him. It had to be connected to the fraught little scene with Sandra. He'd been fine until then, genial, amusing, putting himself out to be a good host. It was only afterwards that he'd clammed up and withdrawn into himself.

At the house, he left the car in the drive, and they walked together towards the house, still without speaking. When they were inside the dimly lit front hall,

Melissa stood there watching while Miles locked up, hesitating, debating what to do.

Actually, she was burning with curiosity. Was the old affair going to be rekindled? Or was it another final farewell? Should she ask him about it, give him a chance to talk it out? Or mind her own business and get to bed? In the end, she decided his love-life was really none of her affair, and if she knew Miles he wouldn't welcome any intrusion into his privacy.

He'd finished bolting the door by now, and had turned around, a glum expression darkening his features. She gave him a bright smile. 'Well, I'll say goodnight, Miles. And thank you for the lovely party. I enjoyed it immensely.'

She turned to go, but hadn't got far when she heard his voice behind her, low and steady, but with an underlying note of emotion throbbing in it that was unmistakable.

'That's right,' he said. 'Just run off to your room.'

That did it! So much for pouring oil on troubled waters! She whirled around, put her hands on her hips and glared at him. 'All right, Miles, something's obviously wrong. Are you going to tell me what it is or are you going to make me guess?'

'You want to know what's wrong?' he said in a menacing tone as he walked slowly towards her. 'All right, I'll tell you what's wrong, since you're apparently too dense to figure it out for yourself.' He was directly in front of her now, his hands on his hips, glaring down at her. 'To begin with, I didn't at all like the way you and David were falling all over each other the entire evening.'

That was so far from what she'd expected that she could only stare at him in utter disbelief. 'You must be joking!' she finally managed to exclaim. 'I'm not interested in David. For heaven's sake, he's an old man.'

Miles crossed his arms over his chest and gave her a withering look. 'He happens to be exactly my age,' was the dry reply.

'Oh, really?' she said. She had to stop a moment to suppress a sudden urge to giggle. 'That's funny,' she finally went on in a saccharine tone. 'I don't think of you as old at all. It must be your nasty disposition.'

'Furthermore,' he ploughed on inexorably, ignoring the comment, 'I don't think that dress you've got on was at all appropriate for my secretary. Not only that, it doesn't suit you at all.'

She could hardly believe her ears. 'Well,' she spluttered at last, 'since you're the one who practically *ordered* me to get some new clothes, I hardly think you're in a position to complain about my choice.'

'I didn't tell you to get yourself up like a tart!' he shouted.

'Tart!' she cried. 'You've got a nerve! This dress is a nun's habit compared to the creations your women come up with.'

'*My* women!' he exploded. 'My *women*? I have no women.' She was about to mention Sandra, but he was one jump ahead of her. 'And if you're referring to Sandra, I certainly would never put you in *her* category. I thought you had more sense.'

They stood there glaring at each other for several long, tense moments. Miles seemed to be waiting for her to say something, to defend herself, but she was so angry she couldn't speak. And why should she have to defend herself anyway? Who was he to pass judgement on her? She hadn't done anything wrong. It was almost as though he hated to see her enjoying herself.

Suddenly, it was all too much for her. Every ounce of energy seemed to be leaking away, and she couldn't deal with it. She felt her face begin to crumple, the hot tears to sting behind her eyes. She turned her head quickly, so he wouldn't notice, but one strangled sob escaped her before she was able to take the first stumbling step away from him towards the safety of her own room.

Then, to her utter dismay, one high heel caught in the carpet, and she could feel herself starting to fall. But by then he'd come up behind her and when she felt his hands settle on her shoulders, holding her up, the dam burst and she covered her face in her hands.

'Oh, God, Melissa,' he said. 'Don't. Please don't cry. I'm sorry. I didn't mean it.'

'There's just no pleasing you,' she blubbered. 'I try and try, and you always find fault, no matter what I do.'

'Please,' he begged. 'Please stop. I can't stand to see you cry.'

She whirled around to face him, stamping her foot in sheer frustration. '*You* can't stand it!' she exclaimed hotly through her tears. 'What about me? All you ever think about is yourself, and I'm sick of it.'

'I know, I know,' he said softly. 'I'm a brute, a beast. I should be horsewhipped, tarred and feathered, run out of town on a rail. I'll prostrate myself at your feet if you like. But please, *please*, stop crying!'

She sniffled loudly and looked up at him. The expression on his face was one of such utter agony that it was almost funny. Quickly he reached in the breast pocket of his jacket, drew out a clean white handkerchief and handed it to her. She wiped her eyes, blew her nose, and sighed deeply.

'Listen,' he said, talking fast, his voice low and urgent. 'I think it's time—long past time—for some honesty between us.' He paused briefly, sucked in a deep breath, then went on. 'To tell you the truth, Melissa, when you showed up tonight in that dress, it was all I could do to keep my hands off you. If all those people hadn't been there, I don't think I could have managed it. Then later, when I saw David pawing you——'

'He wasn't pawing me!' she broke in. 'All we did was dance a few times.'

'Call it what you like, it doesn't matter,' he ground out. His eyes were fastened on her, his hands digging into her shoulders. 'All I know is I've never wanted a woman so badly in my life as I wanted you, still want you. Now. This minute.'

Astounded, Melissa raised her eyes to meet his penetrating grey gaze. What she saw there in the silvery depths took her breath away. He meant it! He wasn't angry at her, wasn't criticising her dress or her behaviour. He *wanted* her! A sudden warm rush of intense satisfaction flooded through her and she smiled up at him.

'Oh, Miles,' she said. 'For such a brilliant man, sometimes you can be so dense. Why didn't you say something?'

He raised a hand and ran it over the back of his neck. 'Because I know you, little Melissa,' he said at last with a bleak smile. 'You certainly realise by now that I'm

incapable of making any permanent commitment to a
woman, even to you. And, much as I want you, I know
you'd never settle for less. So what was the point?'

All that mattered to Melissa was that he'd come out
with it at last, actually admitted he wanted her, and this
time he hadn't backed off without a word of explanation. She understood what he was saying, but at the
moment her only certainty was that she wanted him, on
any terms she could get him. The future would just have
to take care of itself.

'Miles?' she said gently. He had turned away from
her, and she put a hand on his cheek, forcing his head
around to face her. 'Miles, don't I have anything to say
about it?'

'What do you mean?' he asked in a tight voice.

'I mean that I'm a grown woman, not a little girl. I
think I have the right to make that kind of decision
myself. And to take responsibility for it.'

He stared down at her thoughtfully for a long moment,
then gave her a crooked grin. 'Better watch out,' he said,
half joking, half serious. 'If you keep on like that you
just might convince me.'

With a laugh, she raised her arms up and threw them
around his neck. 'Oh, Miles. What do you think I've
been trying to do?'

The next thing she knew, his arms had come around
her and he was holding her tightly all along the length
of his hard body. With a low groan deep in his throat
his mouth came down on hers, drawing deeply on her
lips, as though to pull the very soul out of her. She met
him eagerly, revelling in the feel of his mouth on hers,
still faintly tasting of the brandy he'd drunk.

Gradually they moved as one into the living-room, still clinging to each other, their lips pressed together, stopping when they reached the couch. He released her for a moment to shrug off his jacket and loosen his tie, dropping both to the floor at his feet in his eagerness to gather her in his arms again.

This time his embrace was more insistent. His hands moved eagerly over her bare back, then lower to clutch at her hips, forcing her lower body up tightly against his hard need. This unmistakable sign of her power over him filled her with a heady sense of joy. To be so urgently desired by such a man was beyond her wildest dreams.

One hand moved to her breast now, sliding sensuously back and forth over the silky material of her dress, and lingering first on one firm mound, then the other, his fingers playing lightly, teasingly, with each thrusting peak. She was beyond any thought of caution by now. All that mattered was to keep alive the delicious sensations he was arousing in her.

When the hand slid up to pull down the tiny straps of the red dress over her shoulders, and he buried his dark head at her bare breast, she threw her head back, arching her back to bring herself even closer to his seeking mouth.

In a moment he pulled away from her again and began to undo his white shirt, fumbling with the buttons in his haste, his eyes never leaving hers. Impulsively, she reached out a hand and placed it over his.

'Let me,' she whispered.

Wordlessly, he nodded and let his hands fall to his sides. She lingered over each button, savouring the feel of his bare skin beneath her fingers as she went, until the last one was undone. Then she put both palms on his broad chest, sliding them over the smooth skin, the hard muscles, the flat abdomen, even, daringly, dipping slightly below the waistband of his trousers.

Finally, with a groan, he stilled her hands, raising them to his lips and gazing down deeply into her eyes. 'Melissa,' he rasped in a hoarse voice. 'Are you sure?'

She slid her arms around his waist and laid her cheek on his smooth bare chest. 'Oh, yes,' she murmured. 'I'm sure.' She smiled up at him. 'There's just one thing. I want so much to please you, Miles, and I don't quite know——' She broke off, embarrassed, and looked away.

'Come on,' he said in a teasing voice. 'Out with it. What deep, dark secrets have you been keeping from me?'

She raised her eyes to his again. 'Well, it's just that I haven't had much experience. I mean, you may have to teach me...'

She stopped short at the look of horror that suddenly appeared on his face. 'Are you trying to tell me this would be the first time for you?' he demanded.

'W-well, yes,' she faltered. 'But that doesn't matter.'

He dropped his hands from her shoulders as though they had been burned, then bowed his head for a moment, obviously struggling for control. Puzzled, she could only stand there and watch him as he turned and walked slowly away from her towards the sideboard against the wall. Hastily she pulled the straps of her dress back up over her shoulders and took a step towards him.

'Miles,' she said, holding out a hand. 'What's wrong?'

'I'm not sure,' he said in a tight voice. 'But I do think I need a drink. How about you?'

'No—no, thanks,' she replied.

He poured a little brandy into a glass, threw back his head and swallowed it all at once. Then he set the glass down and just stood there for a moment, his back towards her, his shoulders hunched over. Finally he turned and came back to her. He took her by the hand and led her over to the couch.

'Listen,' he said, drawing her down beside him. 'Before this gets really out of hand, we have a few things to discuss.'

'But Miles,' she protested, 'you have to let me decide——'

'It's not that,' he broke in with a wave of his hand. 'I agree, it is your decision, but I do feel a sense of responsibility, considering your—uh—situation. You know. What I'm talking about is the...' He shrugged. 'Well, the practical arrangements.'

'What do you mean?'

'Well, for one thing,' he said with a grin, 'I'll have to find a new secretary.'

'But why? Why can't we just go on as we have?'

He shook his head. 'It won't work. Just listen a minute. I think it would be best if we found you an apartment in town.' When she started to protest, he raised a hand, stopping her. 'I'll pay for it, of course. Don't worry about that.'

'It's not the money,' she said. 'I don't see why I can't just stay on here.'

'Don't you see, darling? It just wouldn't work. If you lived here now, I'd never get any work done.' He put his mouth on her neck just below her ear, nuzzling, and laid a hand on her breast. 'I could never keep my hands off you. You'd be too distracting.'

Melissa felt as though he'd just thrown a bucket of cold water over her. Put in those crass, businesslike terms, the whole affair took on an entirely different aspect, even seemed shoddy. Would she end up like Sandra when he got tired of her?

'What you're saying,' she finally said, 'is that you want me to be your kept mistress.'

His head shot up and he reared back, narrowing his eyes at her. 'That's a rather crude way of putting it,' he said stiffly.

'But it's true, isn't it?'

He got up from the couch and began pacing up and down the room. She sat there, tense and anxious, watching him, until finally he came back to stand before her, his face grave.

'I just don't see any other way,' he said at last in a low voice. 'I've warned you more than once that I couldn't make you any promises, and you assured me it didn't matter.' He sat down beside her and took her hands in his. 'It's up to you, Melissa. You'll have to decide what you want, what you're willing to take responsibility for. I can't make that decision for you. All I can do is be as open and honest with you as possible.'

'I know,' she said. 'It's just that moving out of the house, your setting me up in an apartment...' She shook her head and looked away. 'It all sounds so sordid.'

What she couldn't tell him was how deeply in love with him she was. Obviously he wanted her, desired her, but he didn't love her. What was she to do? She couldn't bear to leave him, but would she be able to tolerate the only way she could keep him?

Finally she withdrew her hands from his and rose slowly to her feet. 'I think if you don't mind I'd like to go to my room now,' she said wearily. 'I'm very tired, and I need to think.'

He stood up beside her. 'Of course. I understand. I'll tell you what. Tomorrow I need to drive into Los Angeles to deliver a copy of the outline to my agent. I'll be back in time for dinner, and we can talk more then. That'll give you time to think it over.'

'All right.'

He put a hand under her chin and tilted her head up to meet his gaze. 'Don't think for a minute that I don't care about you, Melissa. I do, in my way, probably more than I've ever cared for another living soul. But I know my limitations. My work is my life, and I can't let anything interfere with it.'

She wanted to cry out to him, to shake him, to ask him how her love could possibly interfere with his work. It meant a lot to her, too. She'd never do anything to harm that. But she knew it was useless. His convictions were carved in stone. There was no shaking him. She'd just have to decide herself what she really wanted, what she'd be able to live with.

'I know,' she said at last. 'I understand. I'll say good-night now, and we can talk about it tomorrow.'

She turned then and walked away from him, knowing the deep grey eyes were fastened on her every step of the way.

CHAPTER NINE

THE next morning Melissa awoke to a thick fog accompanied by a steady drizzle. After a restless night of tossing and turning in a vain attempt to decide what to do about Miles, she'd finally fallen into an exhausted sleep in the early hours of the morning. Now, the moment she opened her eyes, the answer came to her. She didn't like it, but there was no other way.

By the time she finished showering and dressing, it was past nine o'clock. Miles was probably already gone and wouldn't be back until evening, but there was a lot to do before then.

Maria had left for her morning's shopping, so she had the kitchen to herself, and as she choked down her meagre breakfast she mulled over her financial situation. With virtually no living expenses for the past several months, the handsome salary Miles paid her had lain almost untouched in the bank. Then there was the generous bonus cheque he'd given her on completion of the outline. Together they came to a sizeable sum, enough at least to carry her for a few months until she got settled somewhere and found another job.

After breakfast she went into the study to call Frances, who recognised her voice right away and seemed pleased to hear from her.

'I was wondering, Frances, if I could take you up on your offer of a visit? Just for a few days.'

'Why, of course, Melissa,' was the immediate warm reply. 'I'd love to have you any time. Were you thinking of coming today?'

'Yes, if it's convenient.'

'Well, as I said, come when you can and stay as long as you like. I'll be glad of the company.'

'I'll have to check the bus schedule, but I think they run up the coast fairly often. I'll call you when I get to Monterey.'

'Oh, no need for that. Just show up whenever you get here. I don't have a car, so you'll have to take a taxi.'

After they hung up, Melissa went to her room to pack. She wouldn't be able to take everything, but she could ask Maria to send the rest of her things on when she found a place of her own.

Two hours later, Melissa was on a bus heading north along the coast road towards Monterey, gazing out of the window at the bleak landscape rushing by. The fog was still so thick the ocean was barely visible, but she wasn't in the mood for enjoying the scenery anyway.

The hardest part had been writing the note to Miles. She'd composed half a dozen versions, discarding them all, until she'd finally decided the best way was just a brief note saying she was leaving, was sure he'd understand why, and would send for the rest of her things when she got settled.

She hadn't intended to tell Maria she was leaving for good, but to her amazement the plump, kindly housekeeper had known exactly what was going on. When Melissa had told her she was going to visit a friend of hers for a while, without specifying whom or where or for how long, Maria had only folded her arms across her ample bosom and nodded knowingly.

'Yes,' she'd said. 'It's best for you to go.' Then she'd shaken her head sadly. 'Mr Thatcher, he's a great man, but like a child when it comes to the heart.' Here she'd thumped her chest meaningfully and rolled her eyes heavenwards.

It was four o'clock in the afternoon when the bus pulled into the depot at Monterey. The fog had lifted by now, and although the air was still misty and damp a pale sun was trying to poke through the high, thin layer of clouds still hanging overhead.

Melissa took a taxi to Frances's address, which turned out to be a pleasant street of modest houses, with well-kept small gardens at the front. The driver stopped in front of a pink stucco bungalow with the inevitable red-tile roof. She got out of the cab, paid the driver, and carried her bags up the front path to the door.

Frances had obviously been watching for her, since the door was flung open immediately. After a quick affectionate hug, she bustled Melissa inside.

'Well, Melissa,' she said, standing back and giving her a long, appraising look, 'I must say you're looking well. Your new job must agree with you. I'd hardly have recognised you.'

Since her heart was breaking, this pronouncement astounded her. 'Thanks, Frances. It's been an interesting time for me.'

Frances peered more closely at her. 'You do look a little pale, however. How about it? Are you hungry, or would you like to freshen up and get settled first?'

'I'm awfully tired, Frances,' she said. 'If you don't mind I think I'd like to lie down for a while.'

'All right. Come with me and I'll show you to your room.'

Frances's guest bedroom was small, but furnished cosily, with a small dressing-table and desk. On the narrow bed was a beautiful handmade patchwork quilt. A table stood beside it holding a frilly lamp, and on the walls hung several lovely photographs of Monterey coastal scenes.

'This is lovely, Frances,' Melissa said with a smile.

'Well, you just make yourself at home.' She went to the door. 'I'll leave you now to get some rest. We can have a little supper when you feel up to it.'

When she'd left, closing the door quietly behind her, Melissa slipped off her shoes and lay down on top of the bed. The moment she closed her eyes images of Miles immediately sprang into her mind—Miles sitting at his desk absorbed in his book, how handsome he'd looked at his celebration party last night, the way he'd held her in his arms and kissed her—and her heart ached within her. Even his less pleasant moods seemed endearing to her now.

Finally, the tears came, and after she'd cried herself out she drifted off into an exhausted sleep.

It was dark when she awakened to the sound of a light tapping on the door. She sat bolt upright and turned on the bedside lamp, blinking in the sudden glare.

'Yes,' she called. 'What is it?'

'There's a telephone call for you, dear. A man.'

Miles! she thought, and her spirits soared. But it couldn't be. He didn't know where she was. There was no one else she wanted to talk to, but it wouldn't do to let Frances know that.

'All right,' she called. 'I'm coming.'

She ran to the door in her stockinged feet. Frances showed her to the telephone at the far end of the hall, then tiptoed away, and Melissa picked it up. 'Hello?' she said warily.

'What do you mean running off like that?' It *was* Miles, after all, and he sounded very angry.

She sank down on the chair. 'How did you find me?'

'Simple deduction. There's only one Frances Venable in the Monterey telephone directory, and I'd heard you once discussing a visit with her. Now, why did you leave?'

'You know why.'

'No. You're wrong. I don't,' he snapped. He paused for a moment, then went on in a softer tone, 'I thought we were going to talk about it, Melissa, after you'd had time to think it over.'

'I did think it over, Miles, believe me, over and over again, but I finally realised I just couldn't live with what you had to offer. What was there left for me to do but leave?'

'And what about me?' he demanded hotly. 'Did you give one thought to what your disappearing like that would do to me?'

Visions of Sandra flashed into her mind. 'Oh, you,' she said wearily. 'You'll survive, I'm sure.'

'Well, I call that a pretty shabby, heartless attitude.'

'Call it anything you like. I just couldn't stay with you, and that's all there is to it.' His total absorption in *his* feelings was beginning to irritate her. 'I'm sure you'll be able to find another secretary who meets your demanding expectations.'

'I don't *want* another secretary,' he shouted. 'I want you!'

'Well, why does everything always have to revolve around what *you* want?' she demanded, really angry by now.

'That's not fair, Melissa,' he said in a hurt voice. 'I was just as concerned with your happiness as my own.'

'Oh, Miles, the woods are full of groupies like Sandra, all dying to become the mistress of a famous man. I just don't happen to be one of them.' She was on the verge of tears by now, her voice shaky. 'Please, just leave me alone,' she implored. 'Don't you see? I simply can't be what you want me to be.'

'I don't want to lose you, Melissa,' he said after a long silence. 'But I'm not going to beg.'

Everything in her ached to go back to him, to take him on any terms she could get him. Just the sound of his voice filled her with longing to feel his arms around her once again. But the thought of being tucked away in some apartment, with nothing to do but wait for him to come to her, stiffened her resolve. It would kill her. It was *because* she loved him so much that she couldn't do it.

'I'm sorry, Miles,' she said at last. 'It just wouldn't work. It's too late to come back to work for you now, and I can't be your kept mistress.' She took a deep breath. 'I'm going to say goodbye and hang up now. Please don't call me again.'

She squeezed her eyes shut tight, then slowly lowered the receiver and replaced it on the cradle.

*   *   *

'I don't mean to pry, dear,' Frances said over dinner, 'but it's obvious something's very wrong. If you feel like talking about it, maybe I could help.'

Melissa laid her fork down and stared fixedly at her plate for a few moments. 'Well,' she said, raising her eyes, 'as you've probably guessed, that was Miles on the telephone.'

Frances nodded. 'Yes, and I also gathered that you weren't just here on a visit. You've quit your job.' She hesitated a moment, then went on cautiously, 'I can see that he might be difficult to work for.'

'Oh, he was,' she said. 'But that wasn't the problem. I loved working for him. He's so——' She shrugged. 'I don't know quite how to put it. He's so *alive*!'

Frances frowned. 'Then why...?'

Melissa gave her a friend a bleak look. 'I fell in love with him, that's why!'

'Ah,' Frances said, rolling her eyes. 'I see. And he's so wrapped up in his work he wasn't interested.'

'No, that's not it. If it had been only that I could have tolerated it.' She took a deep breath and plunged ahead. 'He wanted me to be his mistress, set me up in an apartment.'

Frances didn't say anything for a long time. Finally she got up, went over to the counter and poured out two cups of coffee, then brought them back to the table and set them down.

'And that was out of the question, I take it?' she asked carefully. 'I mean, as far as you were concerned?'

'Of *course* it was out of the question!' Melissa cried. 'It's so typical of his arrogance, his blindness where human relationships are concerned! I can't for the life of me understand how a man with such a penetrating mind can be so dense about feelings!'

After that outburst, they sat in silence for a while, drinking their coffee, until finally Frances cleared her throat. 'I gather the telephone call was to ask you to come back?'

'Yes. Can you believe it? He seems to think he can insult me, then calmly ask me to come back to work for him.'

Frances shook her head. 'Can you imagine that? Why, I don't blame you for being furious. He certainly has a nerve!'

Melissa gave her a suspicious look. There was something in her voice that didn't sound quite right. Was she really agreeing with her, or was there a hint of sarcasm there? But Frances only sat there calmly, sipping her coffee, the picture of innocence.

'Well, actually,' Melissa hedged, reddening, 'there's a little more to it than that.'

Frances raised an eyebrow. 'Oh? You know, I'm a little confused here. You say you love him and it's obvious that in his way he must care a lot about you. Yet you speak about him as though he were some old lecher trying to seduce an innocent young girl.'

Melissa could only stare. 'Frances!' she exclaimed at last. 'You're not telling me I should agree to his stupid proposal!'

'No, not exactly. I just don't think that loving a genius would be simple under any conditions. Allowances would have to be made. But perhaps it might be worth it, for the right woman.'

Melissa rose up slowly from her chair. 'Oh, Frances, I don't want to talk about it any more tonight. I'm just dead beat. If you don't mind, I think I'll have a bath and turn in.'

'Of course, dear. By tomorrow it will all be clearer to you.'

But Frances was wrong. Although Melissa was certain in her mind that she was doing the right thing, that she couldn't go back to Miles now under any conditions, her heart didn't agree. The longing for Miles continued to torment her, the doubts to tear her apart.

For the next several days she tried her best to enter into Frances's plans for entertaining her, but her heart wasn't in it. After that first night the subject of Miles Thatcher wasn't raised again, nor did he try to contact her in any way. Jack called once, but she wasn't in the mood for his brand of fun and she put him off.

Then one evening, after she'd been there for a week, she was in the kitchen washing up the dinner dishes when she heard Frances call to her from the living-room, where she was watching the evening news. Her tone was so urgent that Melissa quickly dried her hands and ran to see what was wrong.

'Oh, Melissa!' Frances said excitedly. 'Come and sit down. There's going to be an interview with Miles Thatcher on next.'

Melissa sank slowly down beside her. 'But he never gives interviews,' she said, bewildered. 'Especially after that last...'

'Shh,' Frances hushed her. 'Here it is.'

The screen flashed from the commercial to a shot of Miles sitting behind the desk in his own study. Across from him was a popular talk-show host, a man whose area of expertise lay in putting his subjects at ease rather than confronting them with probing questions. Still, Melissa could hardly believe her eyes.

'First of all, Mr Thatcher,' the man was saying, 'I want to thank you for agreeing to this interview.'

'My pleasure,' Miles murmured.

Melissa almost had to laugh. The look on his face was quite pleasant, but she knew him well enough to realise that underneath the bland façade he was suffering excruciating pain at having his precious privacy invaded, even his own home on exhibit, and she wondered what in the world had made him agree to it.

The interviewer was speaking again. 'Now, Mr Thatcher, we all know you don't like to discuss a book in progress, but would you at least tell our audience a little bit about it?'

'Well, it's set in Mexico. I've always loved the place, and, some months ago, I took a cruise down along the western coast that turned out to have a special personal significance for me.'

'I see,' the man said. He leaned towards Miles avidly, clearly ready to pounce on the opening he'd given him. 'And would you care to elaborate on that statement?'

Melissa snorted. Fat chance of that! Any intrusion into his personal life was strictly off-limits. But then he'd brought the subject up himself, after all, and had only himself to blame. And what did he mean by claiming it had a 'personal significance' for him? She leaned forward, chin in hand, listening intently.

'Well,' Miles replied, 'I met someone on that trip who became very important to me, who changed some of my most basic attitudes.' He scowled darkly then, clearly reluctant to go on. 'In fact,' he muttered at last, 'on one very crucial issue in particular.'

'A woman?' was the eager question. Miles only nodded, but didn't elaborate. After a short silence, the host tried a more oblique attack. 'You've never been married, have you, Mr Thatcher?'

'No,' he replied curtly, shifting uncomfortably in his chair.

The man was looking a little desperate now at having to prise every word out of him. 'Well, are you saying that might change?'

'It might.'

'Because of the person you met in Mexico, I take it.'

Miles only nodded, a look of such patent misery on his face that Melissa's heart went out to him. Gradually, the full import of what he'd done, what he'd said, in front of a television camera, with possibly millions of people watching in, hit her.

In a daze, she heard the interviewer thanking Miles, and then the next commercial appeared. Apparently it was all over. Melissa sat there speechless, still trying to assimilate what she'd just seen and heard, when suddenly the front doorbell rang.

'Would you mind answering that, Melissa?' Frances said. 'I think it might be for you anyway.' She rose to her feet. 'I'll be in my room if you want me.'

Melissa stared blankly after her as she left. What was going on? The bell chimed again. Slowly, she rose to her feet and went out into the front hall to answer the door.

'Hello, Melissa,' Miles said.

She blinked her eyes. 'Miles?' she said in a small voice. 'What are you doing here? We just saw you...'

'Taped,' he said brusquely. 'May I come in?'

Without waiting for an answer, he brushed past her, and she followed him into the living-room. He stood in the middle of the room for a moment, surveying the scene, the television still blaring, then walked over and switched it off.

He turned to face her. 'Ah, so you did watch,' he said with satisfaction. 'Frances said she'd see to that.'

'Frances?' she asked, bewildered. 'You mean you arranged this with Frances?'

He waved a hand in the air. 'Yes, but that doesn't matter. The important thing is that you saw it.'

'Yes, I saw it. But I still don't believe it.' She walked over to him and gazed up into his face. 'Why did you do it, Miles?'

He stood there looking down at her silently for several long moments. 'Why do you think?' he said at last.

'At the moment I'm too confused to think much of anything.'

'*You're* confused!' he exclaimed. 'You know, Melissa,' he said with a sigh, 'I've gone over and over everything that's passed between us, and I still can't figure you out.' His voice hardened. 'Why in God's name did you run off that way? The night of the party you were ready for anything. Then the next thing I knew you were gone. So, what happened to change your mind? Don't you think you owe me that much?'

'Yes,' she said at last, knowing he was right. 'I guess I do.' She thought a moment, then lifted her chin at him. 'I just didn't like the way you put it,' she declared stoutly.

'I mean, you made it seem so cheap, just like a business proposition.'

'Aha!' he said. 'Just as I thought. It wasn't romantic enough for you, right? Well, to answer your question,' he went on without waiting for an answer, *'that's* why I did it.' He pointed to the television set. 'It was the only way I could think of to get through to you. You wouldn't talk to me, wouldn't let me explain.' He shrugged. 'So I decided to go public with my proposal.'

'Proposal?' she asked warily.

'Yes, damn it,' he ground out. 'If the only way I can get you is to marry you, then I guess that's what I'll have to do.'

'Well, if that's your idea of romantic,' she said heatedly, 'I can't say I think much of it. You make it sound like blackmail. I'd never try to force you into something you don't want to do. Just because I can't play according to your rules doesn't mean I'm insisting you play by mine.'

He threw back his head and laughed. 'Do you really think that's possible?' he asked. 'That I'd submit to blackmail?'

She had to smile. 'No,' she replied in a dry tone. 'I guess I lost my head there for a minute.' She gave him a troubled look. 'But you do make it sound as though you're being pushed into something you really don't want. I couldn't live with that.'

He shook his head wearily from side to side and uttered a heartfelt sigh. 'Melissa, what am I going to do with you? Won't anything satisfy you? You don't want to be my secretary, you won't be my mistress, and now you refuse to marry me.' He threw up his hands. 'What *do* you want, for God's sake? What does it take to please you?'

She turned away from him, biting her lip. She knew exactly what she wanted, but he was apparently incapable of giving it to her. She thought about Frances's words that first night—that loving a genius was never simple, but worth it to the right woman. Was she the right woman? Or were her own needs too strong?

Then she felt his arms come around her, his long, lean body pressed against her back, his mouth nuzzling at her cheek. For a split-second she hesitated, then with a sigh of surrender she sank back against him.

He brushed her hair back from her ear and put his lips up close to it. 'Don't you see, darling?' he murmured. 'I only want to please you. Just tell me what it is you want. I'm desperate. I'll do anything you ask.'

Suddenly it came to her that, with all his faults, the moods, the arrogance, the demands he made, he was actually humbling himself to her. Although this filled her with a heady sense of the enormous power she wielded over him, at the same time she knew she must never abuse it. A man like Miles didn't humble easily, and when he did it must mean he cared a great deal, whether he knew it or not.

Slowly she turned around to face him. 'Why, Miles?' she asked softly. 'Why are you doing all this—the interview, the proposal of marriage, coming here to Frances's house?'

He gave her a puzzled look. 'Why? Because I love you, of course. What other reason could there be?'

It was exactly what she'd wanted to hear. 'Oh, Miles,' she cried, throwing her arms around his neck. 'Do you really?'

'Well, of course I do,' he said, laughing and gathering her in his arms. 'Why else do you think I agreed to make such a fool of myself on national television?'

She eyed him narrowly. 'You know, Miles, for such an articulate man you certainly don't have a way with words when it comes to love.'

They clung together for several long moments. She'd never let him get away now, Melissa thought dreamily. Not after he'd declared his intentions to the world. He wouldn't dare. The rasp of his cheek against hers, the familiar clean, masculine scent of his skin and hair, the pressure of his long, hard body against hers, all filled her with such exquisite tenderness for him, such yearning desire, that she could hardly breathe.

Finally, his mouth came down on hers in a long, possessive kiss, but before it could get out of hand he drew back from her. 'Come on,' he said, leading her over to the couch. 'Before we get started on *that*, we've got a lot to talk about.'

'Yes, Miles,' she said meekly.

He pulled her down on to his lap. 'Now,' he said in his old clipped, no-nonsense tone of voice, 'I've looked into all the details. It takes three days to get married in California.' He grinned at her. 'Unless you'd like to take a run across the border and get married in Mexico.'

She stared at him. 'So soon?'

He nodded. 'Why not? Provided, that is, you think you'll be able to put up with my difficult temperament.

My ''nasty disposition'', I think you called it once,' he added drily.

'Sorry about that,' she murmured. 'I take it all back.'

Married to Miles! She wouldn't have to leave his house! Even with all her lingering doubts, she'd been ready today to agree to anything, and now he'd resolved them all in one stroke. Still, she had to make sure. She gave him a troubled look.

'Miles, are you sure this is what you want? I mean, what about your convictions that marriage would interfere with your work?'

He shrugged. 'Well, so I've changed my mind. Haven't you heard? ''A foolish consistency is the hobgoblin of little minds'',' he quoted. 'That's Emerson. It takes a stronger character to admit one's mistakes than it does to cling to them. Besides the fact that I can't live—or work—without you, I rather like the idea of settling down into connubial bliss. I can even envision several little Thatchers in our future.'

She laughed happily. 'Not too many, I hope.'

'As many as you want, darling,' he said in a low voice. 'I'm putty in your hands.'

She seriously doubted that, but it wouldn't hurt to let him think it. 'Well, then,' she said, nestling closer to him, 'we'll wait and see how the first few turn out.'

'Now,' he went on, settling back and drawing her head down on his shoulder, 'where do you want to go on our honeymoon?'

She didn't even have to think. 'I want to go home,' she stated emphatically. His house was the first real home she'd known since her parents died. It was where she belonged.

*　　*　　*

On Saturday evening, three days later, they were married at Miles's house, with Maria, Pedro, David and Frances in attendance. Melissa had stayed with Frances in those intervening days, at Miles's insistence, and the two women had driven down to Santa Barbara together in a rented car.

After the ceremony and a short celebration supper, Miles made it crystal-clear that he expected everyone to leave immediately, practically shooing them out of the door when they'd swallowed their last bite. Frances was staying in a hotel in town, at Miles's expense, and would drive back to Monterey the next day, and he'd given Maria and Pedro the night off.

When all the guests had gone, the front door closed behind them, Miles turned to Melissa, radiant in her white satin wedding dress, the short veil framing her face.

'God,' he said with feeling, 'I thought they'd never leave.'

Melissa laughed. 'After the way you hinted around all evening I'm surprised they stayed as long as they did.'

As he walked slowly towards her, the gleam in the silvery eyes an unmistakable indication of what was on his mind, Melissa held her breath, waiting.

'Well, Mrs Thatcher,' he said softly. 'Alone at last.' He reached out a hand to remove the veil from her head and set it down on a nearby table. 'You make a beautiful bride.'

'I'm glad you think so.''

He put a hand on her face. 'Any regrets, darling?'

'Oh, no,' she replied, shaking her head vigorously. 'How about you?'

He gave her a slow, lazy smile, and the hand on her face slid down to grasp the base of her neck. 'Not so far,' he murmured. 'You know, we omitted an important part of the ceremony.'

'Oh? What's that?'

'Since we were married in the house, I never got a chance to carry you over the threshold.'

'Well,' she said evenly, her eyes never leaving his, 'it's not too late, is it?'

Wordlessly, he scooped her up in his strong arms and carried her down the hall towards the bedroom wing. Melissa put her arms around his neck and nestled her head on his broad shoulder, not really sure where he was taking her, but not caring much either.

She'd never been inside his bedroom, only seen glimpses of it going down the hall. It was quite a large room, starkly masculine, decorated in cool shades of grey and blue, and looking out on to a small private terrace. He set her down beside the bed, then switched on the lamp beside it.

In his shirt-sleeves now, his tie loosened, he turned back to her. 'Nervous?' he asked with a smile.

She shook her head. 'Not a bit.' It was true. She was in a state of total bliss, as though she'd died and gone to heaven.

Then it dawned on her that *he* was a little edgy, and she had to smile. In many ways he was such a child. Here was a man with a long, colourful history of romantic experience, nervous on his wedding night. Her deep love for him, her infallible feminine instinct, told her exactly what to do about it.

She walked over to him, put her arms around his waist and looked up into his eyes. 'I love you, Miles,' she whispered.

'And I love you, darling.' His voice was husky and throbbing with unconcealed emotion.

His arms came around her then, holding her tightly, as though afraid she'd vanish if he let go. Melissa sank against him, floating mindlessly, carried away by an overpowering desire for this man. His hand was moving up and down her bare arm in a soothing, hypnotic rhythm, and she laid her head on his shoulder with a sigh.

Slowly he lowered his head. She closed her eyes, waiting, and when his lips touched hers a deep joy filled her. His mouth was soft, brushing lightly over hers in a slow, sensuous motion at first. Then, suddenly, as though they both burst into flame at once, they clung together blindly in a frantic embrace.

Eagerly she pressed herself up against him, clutching at the back of his neck, raking her fingers through the crisp, dark hair. His hands moved to the back opening of her dress, fumbling with the fastening, then pulling it off her shoulders and down to her waist.

Wordlessly, still locked together, they sank down on the edge of the bed. As his kiss became more urgent, she lowered her head back to rest on the pillows. He leaned over her, his hot tongue probing and insistent, demanding entrance. With no thought except for him, she surrendered to him totally.

As his tongue explored her mouth, his hands moved over her body possessively from her shoulders to her breasts, then down to her thighs, as though he wanted to memorise every inch of her. His touch on her skin sent a shaft of liquid fire coursing through her blood, and she moaned faintly, closing her eyes and sighing deeply when his hands came back up to close around her breasts.

'God, what you do to me, Melissa,' he breathed harshly. He raised his head, his grey eyes glittering down at her. 'There hasn't been a day since we first met that I haven't wanted you.'

He pulled away from her for a moment to unbutton his shirt and shrug it off, then came back, trailing his long fingers down her arm and bending his head to lay his lips on her bare shoulder.

'Touch me,' he murmured.

Eagerly, she reached out to run both hands lightly over the lithe, sinewy muscles of his strong arms and broad, smooth chest. As her fingers trailed lower, fluttering on his flat abdomen, he sucked in a deep breath, and she could feel the muscles quivering under her touch. He reached behind her then to unclasp her lacy white bra and slipped it off. She tensed up, a little self-conscious about her slim figure, hoping he wouldn't be disappointed.

He sat there gazing at her for a long moment. 'You're as beautiful as I knew you'd be,' he said with wonder in his voice.

He placed a hand over one bare breast, then the other, moving back and forth lightly, barely touching. Then he bent his head and opened his lips over one taut, thrusting peak, drawing on it, flicking his tongue over it, while his hands slid lower.

She was filled with a wild elation, a mindless ecstasy, barely able to suppress a glad cry of joy as she clutched at the dark head at her breast. With a low groan deep in his throat, he left her again to shed the rest of his clothing.

Then, after one last long, lingering caress, his breath coming in great racking gasps, he covered her body with his, and they became one at last, joined together in the deepest expression of love between a man and a woman.

Some time later Melissa lay beside her husband, watching him sleep, listening to his deep, steady breathing, and gazing her fill at the long, lithe body lying next to her, half covered by the tangled sheet. His head was turned away, his strong features in profile, the long, thick lashes resting on the bony cheeks, a lock of tangled hair falling over his forehead.

A great surge of love for him rose up in her, so powerful that she could barely contain it. This man is my husband, she thought. He belongs to me. She knew there would be difficulties ahead, that dealing with such a complex man was not going to be easy, but with a little luck and a lot of love her own more stable nature would be enough to carry her through anything.

She lay dreamily back on the pillow, her thoughts returning to the first time they'd met, on the trip to Mexico. She'd come such a long way since then. The shy, mousy little girl had become a woman at last. Just then she became aware of a large warm hand snaking around her waist and sliding up to cover her breast.

'Mmm,' she heard him murmur sleepily. 'You feel good lying next to me when I wake up.'

'Miles,' she said, turning to him. 'Remember when you asked me where I wanted to go on our honeymoon?'

'Mmm-hmm,' he replied, his hand travelling lower.

'Well, I've decided. I want to take another trip to Mexico.'

'Anything you say, darling,' he replied, his caresses becoming more insistent.

Sighing with pleasure, she turned into his arms and nestled up against him. With Miles beside her as her husband, a second cruise to Mexico really would be a voyage to enchantment.

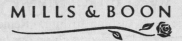

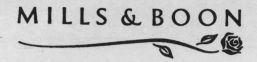

MILLS & BOON

Next Month's Romances

Each month you can choose from a wide variety of romance with Mills & Boon. Below are the new titles to look out for next month.

THE SHINING OF LOVE	Emma Darcy
A BRIEF ENCOUNTER	Catherine George
SECRET OBSESSION	Charlotte Lamb
A VERY SECRET AFFAIR	Miranda Lee
DEAREST LOVE	Betty Neels
THE WEDDING EFFECT	Sophie Weston
UNWELCOME INVADER	Angela Devine
UNTOUCHED	Sandra Field
THIEF OF HEARTS	Natalie Fox
FIRE AND SPICE	Karen van der Zee
JUNGLE FEVER	Jennifer Taylor
BEYOND ALL REASON	Cathy Williams
FOREVER ISN'T LONG ENOUGH	Val Daniels
TRIUMPH OF LOVE	Barbara McMahon
IRRESISTIBLE ATTRACTION	Alison Kelly
FREE TO LOVE	Alison York

GET 4 BOOKS AND A MYSTERY GIFT

Return the coupon below and we'll send you 4 Mills & Boon romances absolutely FREE! We'll even pay the postage and packing for you.

We're making you this offer to introduce you to the benefits of Reader Service: FREE home delivery of brand-new Mills & Boon romances, at least a month before they are available in the shops, FREE gifts and a monthly Newsletter packed with information.

Accepting these FREE books places you under no obligation to buy, you may cancel at any time, even after receiving just your free shipment. Simply complete the coupon below and send it to:

HARLEQUIN MILLS & BOON, **FREEPOST**, PO BOX 70, CROYDON CR9 9EL.

Yes, please send me 4 Mills & Boon romances and a mystery gift as explained above. Please also reserve a subscription for me. If I decide to subscribe I shall receive 6 superb new titles every month for just £11.40* postage and packing free. I understand that I am under no obligation whatsoever. I may cancel or suspend my subscription at any time simply by writing to you, but the free books and gift will be mine to keep in any case. *I am over 18 years of age.*

NO STAMP NEEDED

1EP5R

Ms/Mrs/Miss/Mr _____

Address _____

_____

_____ Postcode _____

Temptation

Lost Loves

'Right Man...Wrong time'

All women are haunted by a lost love—a disastrous first romance, a brief affair, a marriage that failed.

A second chance with him...could change everything.

Lost Loves, a powerful, sizzling mini-series from Temptation continues in April 1995 with...

**Even Cowboys Get the Blues
by Carin Rafferty**

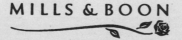

MILLS & BOON